'Don't say it. Don't say u — word – that ugly name screamed at his father day from the hatred and fury of the picket line . . .

A scab! That's how Tom Farrell's father is branded – and Tom is made to suffer for it. Yet even in his isolation, Tom senses the strength and the independence that come from doing what you believe in. And this same quality brings him a new friend and ally – ironically, from the heart of the other side. Melanie Wall's father is the leader of the strike. Like Tom, Melanie is behind *her* father, but she knows that the right to disagree with the majority is precious, and must be protected at all costs.

Theirs is an uneasy friendship at times; and made all the more difficult by the divided community in which they live. Yet, on the night when both Tom and Melanie discover a treacherous plot which threatens both their families, they have to take swift and united action.

Bel Mooney was born and brought up in Liverpool, but moved to the West Country when she was fourteen. After University she became a well-known journalist and travelled all over England, writing features about British children and the way they live. *A Flower of Jet* is her sixth children's book; she also writes novels for adults, and appears on television and radio. Bel Mooney is married with two children.

Also by Bel Mooney

THE STOVE HAUNTING

A FLOWER OF JET

Bel Mooney

PUFFIN BOOKS

PUFFIN BOOKS

Published by the Penguin Group
Penguin Books Ltd, 27 Wrights Lane, London w8 5tz, England
Viking Penguin, a division of Penguin Books USA Inc.
375 Hudson Street, New York, New York 10014, USA
Penguin Books Australia Ltd, Ringwood, Victoria, Australia
Penguin Books Canada Ltd, 2801 John Street, Markham, Ontario, Canada l3r 1b4
Penguin Books (NZ) Ltd, 182–190 Wairau Road, Auckland 10, New Zealand

Penguin Books Ltd, Registered Offices: Harmondsworth, Middlesex, England

First published by Hamish Hamilton Children's Books 1990
Published in Puffin Books 1991
1 3 5 7 9 10 8 6 4 2

Printed in England by Clays Ltd, St Ives plc
Filmset in Baskerville

For Daniel and Kitty

This book belongs to

Selena Halliday

CHAPTER ONE

Melanie couldn't sleep. At first she was too cold, then too hot; she tossed about and her quilt slipped to the floor ... and as she bent crossly to pull it back she heard the voices again.

Each night now for over a week it had been the same. Instead of the comforting chatter of the television in the sitting room below, and then the familiar noises of the kettle being filled, the fire raked and her parents preparing for bed – there was this other sound. Talking. That's all. And yet it worried Melanie. It was not the idle conversational buzz she was used to. This talking was different: low, fierce and tense. It pulled at her mind like a dark, underwater current – worrying her, although she could not say why.

She slid from her bed, and crouched with her ear to the floor. They were not quarrelling – she knew that. Melanie's parents both had quick tempers (as Melanie did herself), and so their rows were short and sharp and soon forgotten. Melanie could only remember them talking in this odd, low tone once before. That was when her big brother Darren was still at school, and frequently in trouble for his loutish behaviour – and truancy.

They had weathered that patch of family trouble.

Darren was a happy-go-lucky young face worker at the mine – at last. But now there was this.

What, though? Through the floor, Melanie could just make out muffled words like 'trouble' and 'hardship' and 'fight'. It was frustrating. So she pulled on her dressing gown and opened her bedroom door, very quietly. She was just tiptoeing down the stairs when the front door opened with a crash. It was Darren – a broad grin on his round face. 'You still up, Mel? I've had a great night, I have! Guess what, Sharon's said she'll go out with me. After all this time!'

The living-room door opened, and Mrs Wall looked out. Before she was sent back upstairs Melanie noticed how her mother *made* the smile on her face. It did not grow there from within; it was deliberately placed.

In the morning, over the usual rushed breakfast, Melanie tried direct tactics.

'Mum – you and Dad were talking ever so late last night. Is something . . .'

'You'll be late for school, love,' was the quick reply.

'Who cares? You didn't answer my question!' said Melanie sharply.

'*I* care. Now go!' There was no jokiness in her mother's voice.

Melanie Wall knew the village street as well as she knew her own face in the mirror. If she closed her eyes she could picture it clearly: long and straight with shops each side, and the skeleton shape of the pit-head gear in the distance – dominating the skyline as it dominated the lives of Mainthorpe people. Chemist, greengrocer's, butcher's, fancy goods store, a tatty supermarket, the bakery where her mother worked, the working-men's club, one or two other shops, the small library . . . that's all there was, really. Nothing to Mainthorpe except this one long street, with the little rows of terraced houses running off each side like ribs. And the pubs. The Red Lion and the Miner's

Lamp stood at each end of the High Street, as if guarding the village from the outside world.

Shoving her hands deep in her coat pockets, Melanie hunched her shoulders against the cold. It was March; a chill breeze blew down the street from the misty hills. The time of daffodils and Easter eggs seemed far away, even though Melanie's father kept rubbing his hands and announcing that it would soon be spring.

But just lately, Melanie thought, his good temper had seemed ... well, it was hard to put a word to it ... *false*, really. And Melanie knew, by instinct, that his moodiness was connected with those low, worrying conversations she heard at night.

'Hey up, Mel.'

'Hey up, Jackie.'

Her best friend fell into step beside her and they walked for a while in silence. There was a sound of running feet behind them.

'Hey up, Wallsie.'

'Wall-y, you mean. Wallsie's a wally!'

Jackie raised her eyes to the heavens as the two boys pushed past them, shouting in voices that were rough yet squeaky at the same time.

'Some people never grow up,' Melanie called after them.

'Take no notice, Mel,' said Jackie.

'Lads in our class, they're so *young*,' shrugged Melanie contemptuously.

'Mm – but that Lofty's quite good-looking,' said Jackie thoughtfully.

'You! You'd think a lamp-post was good-looking, if it had trousers on!' jeered Melanie.

Jackie flicked back her long fair hair. 'Just 'cos you're a tomboy, Melanie Wall!'

The village street was full of girls and boys like them, drifting to school, wearing a variety of coats in the regulation colours of grey or navy. Dark shapes

3

against the grey stone buildings, they walked slowly, dragging their clumpy feet in the heavy lace-up shoes that were fashionable for both sexes. The shoes made legs look thin and spindly; once their art teacher had shown them a picture by an artist called Lowry and Form 3C had laughed at the little stick figures with big feet under a grey sky, not recognizing themselves at all.

With all their schoolmates, the girls turned right at the Red Lion and surveyed the flat, grey-green roofs and glassy walls of their school, the Ernest Bevin Comprehensive. Pupils were streaming through the gates, most of them sighing inwardly, as Melanie was, at the thought of another whole week at school.

'I don't like Mondays,' said Jackie.

'English isn't bad.' Melanie was the kind of girl who could not stay gloomy for long; there was something good about most days, she thought.

Just then, as they approached the school gates, the girls were overtaken by a heavily-built boy their own age, who swung an army surplus bag full of books over one shoulder. His hair was cut in the same style as most of the other boys': short at the sides and standing up like a nailbrush on top. Like them he wore a flimsy dark blue bomber jacket, and had turned up the legs of the regulation grey school trousers to display his heavy Doctor Martens boots.

But Melanie always thought there was something different about Tom Farrell. His face, turning now to grin broadly at them, was . . . nice-looking (yes, all the girls thought so) but something more important than that . . . It was *kind*.

'Aren't you going to wait for us, Tom?' Jackie called, quickening her pace.

'Be late,' he said casually, slowing down nevertheless. They caught up, and the three of them walked for a few yards in silence.

'What's the matter – cat got your tongue?' Melanie asked at last, glancing sideways at Tom.

'It's nothing. Not much, anyway,' Tom frowned.

'That French we had to do last night was really bad,' sighed Jackie. 'And the TV was on so loud I couldn't hear myself think.'

'Don't give us that, Jackie, you don't *think*!' said Tom, as if making an effort to be light-hearted.

'I don't think in *French*, right enough.' Jackie tossed her head.

Melanie was quiet. There was something wrong with Tom. She knew it. Somehow or other, she put it together with the something that was wrong at home. And suddenly she felt a spurt of anger, as well as frustration. If there was a secret, then there was no reason why she should not share it.

'There's going to be trouble,' Tom said suddenly, closing his mouth tight as soon as the words were out.

'What do you mean?' Melanie asked.

'Heard my dad talking to one of his mates last night. You know they were talking about closing the pit?'

'In *Mainthorpe*?', said Jackie incredulously.

Melanie knew. All the fragments fell together in her mind at last, and now she saw that *this* must be the reason for those late, whispered conversations.

Tom went on. 'Dad says they've got a secret plan to close pits all over the country. He says it'll happen, sure enough, and no one can stop it. They've got a union meeting tonight. Going to vote.'

'On what?' asked Jackie.

'Must be on a strike, you daft thing,' said Melanie. She only had a vague idea of what that would mean. Dad and Darren wouldn't go to work, of course – but then, what would they do for money? But her moment's anxiety was banished by Jackie's little whoop of excitement.

'At least it'ud be something *happening* in boring old

Mainthorpe,' her friend said, as they rushed in through the huge glass doors, and heard the first bell.

There was a scuffle going on in the boys' cloakroom when Tom went to hang up his jacket, but he barely turned to look. It happened all the time: name-calling and pushing and shoving and small fights. It was as if the boys his age were so full of energy that this was the only way they could show it – by fighting, forming small gangs, arguing within the gangs, and occasionally even going out to smash up a fence or whatever happened to be in their way.

There was no real harm in any of it, he knew that. Nobody ever got hurt; there was just this feeling they all seemed to share, that you had to act tough. By the time they got to sixteen most of them changed – thinking of work, of going to the pub every Friday and Saturday, of being men. There was no sixth form at the school. Each year about twenty out of the two hundred leavers went on to the sixth form college in Mexton, a few more took typing or catering courses, and the rest went to work. The girls would go to work in shops, factories and offices in Sheffield, Rotherham and Doncaster; the boys would become miners like their fathers.

Or not. 'We want you to do all the things we never did,' said his parents about twice a week, driving him mad. 'You'll be able to go to University, get away from here, get a good job.' That was his father's line.

'He'll do well for himself, our Tom,' said his mother fondly, talking to friends and neighbours as if he wasn't there.

His brother Jason would light a cigarette, and laugh, and draw a halo in the air over his head, winking at Tom. The wink wasn't always friendly: it was a squint at the huge difference between the brothers. Jason was seventeen, and a miner, like their father. 'Ah, *he's* the brainy one,' he said mockingly one day, jerking a thumb at Tom as if he was an alien creature. '*He* won't be getting his hands dirty like me.'

Sometimes Tom would talk about jobs with his two close friends, Eddy Smith and Lee Douglas.

'Waste of time talking about the future,' said Eddy, ''cos what'll happen will happen, fast enough.'

'Your dad's right though, Tom,' said Lee. 'You've got the brains, lad!'

'What'll *you* do then?' he asked them.

'Go down the pit, of course,' was the confident reply.

The cloakroom was emptying. Eddy and Lee came up each side of him from the front, linking their arms through his and dragging him along backwards.

Eddy gave him a playful punch as they let him go. 'Old Skinny'll skin you alive, Tom! Standing there miles away, and the last bell's gone.'

Mr Skinner, their form-master, frowned as the three boys rushed in and took their places, but he continued with the register. 'Lee Douglas.'

'H-h-h-ere, s-s-s-s-sir,' clowned Lee, exaggerating his shortness of breath.

'Tom Farrell.'

'Heah, SAH!' barked Tom, like a sergeant-major.

Mr Skinner's frown deepened, but he said nothing. Melanie grinned at Jackie.

Mr Skinner was a thin man in his fifties who looked just like his name, and he rarely smiled. He took the first lesson, which was Tom's favourite subject – English. This morning Tom found concentration impossible, and the whole class was more restless than usual.

When the bell rang for the end of the lesson, Mr Skinner told Tom to wait behind for a few moments. 'Here you are, Farrell,' he said, holding out a folded piece of paper. 'I thought this might interest you.' Tom took it, and read what it said on the front. A national chain of large bookshops was holding an essay competition for school pupils, with prizes of

7

money for the winners themselves and for their schools. 'Why don't you have a go, Farrell? I'd say you stand a reasonable chance,' said Mr Skinner, in a tone that was unusually approving.

'I'll think about it, sir,' said Tom, shoving the entry form in his pocket.

At break the kids stood about. There was the usual noise, of course, and the first years ran about kicking balls, and generally making a nuisance of themselves. But the older ones huddled in small groups, talking. Everybody seemed to know about the big meeting that was to be held that night.

'There'll be a strike.'

'Our dad says it's now or never. The gaffers want to smash the union.'

'There'll be some scraps!' – this said with great glee.

'That government, they don't know how the other half lives – that's what our mum says.'

'Aye, that's right. Should come up here, they should.'

But after a few minutes the talk drifted to other matters. The pupils at Ernest Bevin Comprehensive knew about mining; they were brought up with talk of 'beltmen', 'chocks', 'boom rippers' and 'gates', and though most of them had never visited the coal face they each had a vivid picture of seams so narrow that a man had to lie on his side to extract the coal, and of long windy tunnels underground that were sometimes cold, sometimes unbearably hot. Knowing all this as they did from the time they were born, it was not interesting to them. The pit was just *there*, like the trees on the hillsides, and the television sets in their living rooms. You didn't think about it at all.

But if it were to close . . .?

Bigger boys shook their heads wisely. 'They'll manage that . . . Hey, what did you think of the match on Saturday?'

Melanie had something else on her mind, in any case. As the day wore on (French, Maths, Music, English . . . all boring, she thought, especially today) she became more and more nervous.

It was The Perm. For weeks now she had been pestering her mother to pay for the new hairstyle she longed for, pouting at her own reflection and pulling scornfully at her straight brown hair. 'Curls, I'd look better with curls,' she said, 'Oh, *please*, Mum!' She was fed up with looking like a tomboy, and wanted a change.

So two hours after school had finished she was staring at herself in the mirror. Little curls stood out all round her face. Was that how she wanted it to be? It was peculiar to see herself without that heavy straight fringe, and for a moment she wanted to cry at her own ugliness. But the hairdresser told her it looked pretty, and when she walked out into the street Melanie felt like someone else, someone older. No one would recognize this new self, she thought, throwing her head back.

'Hey up, Melanie, what've you done to your hair?'

It was Tom Farrell, carrying a couple of library books.

'Ask a stupid question, Tom Farrell,' she snapped, feeling nervous and stupid again.

'Looks like you been eating your crusts!' he grinned. 'Your mother'll turn you upside down and use you to scour the step.'

'Huh, *your* mother could use you to clean her shoes,' Melanie retorted, pointing at his bristled hair.

He took no notice. Still smiling he reached out a hand and touched her hair. 'Feels just like a brillo pad,' he said.

Melanie had a quick temper. 'Oh you shut up, Farrell,' she shouted, feeling tears well in her eyes as she turned angrily away.

He caught her up. 'Don't be so daft, Melanie. I didn't mean nothing. It looks right nice, if you want to know.'

'No, it doesn't,' she said in a small voice.

'It does, Mel. It looks nicer than it did, it really suits you – honest.'

'Huh.'

'Don't be like that.'

They walked in silence for a few moments. Then across the road Melanie saw Mick Golding, the young policeman, and she grinned. Uncle Mick, as she called him, wasn't really her uncle, he was her mother's cousin. But whenever he and his wife Angie came to their house they always brought Melanie chocolates. She loved chocolates, and it was hard to see Uncle Mick in his uniform without thinking about them. Last Christmas she had given him a chocolate policeman, wrapped in shiny blue foil.

Now he seemed to be looking at her, but he didn't call out, or wave as she expected him to. He looked different, somehow. Worried.

Suddenly Melanie stopped thinking about her hair. When she called out to Mick he raised his hand absent-mindedly, without a smile. It wasn't like him at all.

Men were walking along the street and going into the Working Men's Club. It was nearly time for the big meeting. Melanie shivered, feeling the wind brush the back of her neck where the hair lay lightly now.

'I wonder what'll happen,' she said.

'My dad says they're bound to vote for a strike,' Tom said, adding, 'Hey, Mel, shall we go and spy on them? Find out what's happening?'

'We can't.'

'Why not?'

'All right, then.' Suddenly Melanie felt a burning need to understand what was going on. If some strange new thing was going to enter their lives, she wanted to be in on it – right from the beginning.

Casually they walked along the road until they reached the plain red-brick house that contained the Mainthorpe Working Men's Club. There was a small alley down the side of the building, and they darted into it. Flattening themselves against the wall, they watched as another group of men went in.

'This is like being little kids,' whispered Melanie.

'Nothing wrong with that,' Tom grinned.

Melanie started to giggle helplessly at the silliness of it. 'Why are we hiding?' she whispered.

''Cos it's more fun than being seen,' he hissed back.

They walked to the back of the building, carefully avoiding two or three dustbins, and stood in the yellow light that filtered through the frosted glass windows. There was a noise from inside, a hubbub of men's voices talking and arguing. Gradually they fell silent, as someone's voice was raised, telling them that the meeting was about to begin.

'We can't see,' Melanie complained.

'We can hear plenty,' said Tom, pointing to the opened metal windows at the top. They could see shadowy shapes against the glass, too, where men and boys were obviously sitting along the window-sills.

'Must be packed in there,' said Melanie.

'Ssssh.'

Voices droned on changing in quick succession, but at last one spoke that was clearer and more powerful that all the others. '*Now listen to me men . . . all of us knew this day would come. We've got to face the truth now and there's no place to hide . . .*'

Tom was looking at Melanie. 'It's my dad!' she said, her eyes wide. He nodded.

'*This decision is the most important one we've ever made about our future. Men have been laid off, we've been treated* with contempt, they've been trying to provoke us for months. And what are we going to do about it?'

There was a small roar, as if an engine was starting to kick to life. But one voice yelled, 'There's nothing we *can* do and you know it.'

'*That's the coward's approach. You want us to take what they dish out to us? You want us to sit back while they destroy our pits and our communities? Well I tell you, I'll not sit back! And I tell you something else. This isn't just a fight for Mainthorpe. It's a fight for whether or not we have a union. Well, let me tell you, lads* ... (Mr Wall's voice had dropped to a menacing whisper now, then rose up to a shout) *I'LL NOT SIT BACK. I'LL FIGHT AND EVERY MAN IN THIS ROOM WORTH CALL-ING A MAN WILL STAND UP SHOULDER TO SHOULDER AND FIGHT WITH ME!'*

At that there was a roar, as if the engine had been turned up full throttle.

'For God's sake man, what are we fighting? It's a losing battle, and we all know it in our hearts.' It was that other voice, the one that had disagreed at first, but it was drowned now by angry shouts.

'*All right, lads. This is a proper meeting and anyone's got the right to speak.*' Melanie had never heard her father sound so serious and strong, and she was astonished. She looked at Tom, wanting him to say something in praise of her dad, but his face was set and pale in the darkness.

There were small groans of protest, and one or two jeers, but the other voice still spoke out clearly. 'All I've got to say is this. Our leaders want us to call a strike now. But it's Spring, and it'll soon be summer, and nobody wants coal in the summer anyway. It's plain daft and anyone can see it. We can't win. If we vote to strike now we'll just be committing suicide.'

'Committing suicide if we don't!'

'Chuck him out!'

'Go back home!'

Whatever else the man was saying was drowned by jeers.

Then Mr Wall's voice cut through again, crisp and clear. '*Now, brothers, we've heard that and we know what we think of it. This is the last ditch battle of our union and if we make a mistake now we'll have it on our consciences for the rest of our lives. We'll be on the dole queues and our sons will be on the dole queues. Forever! IT'S NOW OR NEVER, LADS. THE FIGHT HAS STARTED. LET'S GET INTO IT – NOW.*'

It seemed as if the walls of the old building would burst with the cheering. Melanie's eyes were bright with pride as she smiled happily at Tom. But he grabbed her arm, avoiding her eyes. 'Come on, let's get out of here.'

'Don't you want to hear the rest?' she asked, running to keep up with him.

'Nothing else to hear,' he said shortly.

Out on the main street Melanie half-ran, half-danced along beside Tom. She did not notice the four or five policemen, Mick Golding amongst them, who now stood across the road in a line, watching the Club.

'Oh, wasn't that fantastic?' she bubbled happily. 'I never knew my dad could talk like that. Like someone on telly – that's what he was. Wasn't he, Tom?'

'Oh, yes, he was great all right,' said Tom quietly, looking at Melanie with an expression she did not understand.

Something in his voice made Melanie bristle. 'What's wrong with what my dad was saying? He's right, isn't he?' Her voice rose a little.

Tom shook his head sadly. 'You don't get it, Melanie. Don't you know who that was in there, disagreeing with your dad? The one they were jeering at?'

Melanie shook her head.

'It was *my* dad,' said Tom.

CHAPTER TWO

The pigeon shed was dark, and full of little cooing sounds. Tom felt the birds moving in the darkness, settling themselves comfortably on their perches. He liked the way they fluffed up the feathers around their necks like ruffs, and huddled down, accepting the human who stood amongst them. They knew him, and they knew his dad. Jason was never so interested, not even when he was younger.

'You're all right in here, you are,' he whispered, stretching out a hand to cup a small soft head very, very gently. The bird moved under his touch. 'Nice and safe in your little house, and nobody can hurt you, that they can't,' Tom went on, in a sing-song, cooing voice that echoed the bird sounds. 'I wish I was you, do you know that? Nothing to worry about . . .'

Tony Farrell's pigeons had won cups, and Tom was as proud of them as his father was. It was more than a hobby. Whenever he felt angry with the world, or just plain miserable, or even only a tiny bit worried about something, he would cross the small yard behind their house and go into the pigeons. That was why he was there this morning, before breakfast.

'Tom! Tom!'

He heard his mother calling from the kitchen door, and realized he was hungry.

The small kitchen was so clean and neat you would not think anyone had cooked breakfast in it. Mr Farrell had built the breakfast corner, with a bench running round two sides, padded with dark red plastic. He had made the white formica table, too, that just fitted into the corner. Red and white tiles, a pile of gleaming stainless steel pans on their stand, mugs hanging from little brass hooks underneath the cupboards ... Their kitchen was one of the nicest in Mainthorpe. Or so Tom thought, sliding into his place at the table. His father and brother had already left for their shift; his eight-year-old sister Linda was dipping bread 'soldiers' into her boiled egg.

'Mum?' said Tom, as his bacon was placed before him.

'Yes, love?'

'How was Jason this morning?'

His mother looked down. 'As sulky as you'd expect.'

'Why sulky?' piped Linda. Tom told her to eat her egg.

Last night he had finally pushed his head under the pillow to blot out the angry sounds. His older brother Jason was shouting at their father. 'I don't have to do anything you say. I don't want to work if my mates are on strike.'

'While you're under my roof, you'll do as I tell you!' was the reply, all the more threatening for being said quietly. And when at last Jason came up to the bedroom the two boys shared he would not speak to Tom at all, but swore under his breath and turned his back.

Suddenly Tom's mother banged her cup down on the table, slopping tea on its surface. 'Oh, I *hate* all this,' she cried.

Tom stared. It was so unlike his mother to spill tea on the table she wiped several times a day that the sick feeling came back to his stomach. It had been there last night. He had woken up with it, but the pigeons had nearly driven it away. Now it was there again – the feeling that something was going to hurt you and there was nothing you could do to stop it.

When Linda went upstairs to clean her teeth, Tom patted his mother's arm awkwardly. 'It'll be all right, Mum,' he said.

She sighed. 'I just feel so wound up inside. Your dad says he'll not go on strike, because he doesn't believe in it. I know he's right, but . . .'

'But what?'

'Neighbours won't like it.'

'It's none of their business,' said Tom, setting his jaw stubbornly in a way that reminded Mrs Farrell of his father.

She sighed again. 'I know it's not, but we all have to live together in a place like Mainthorpe, and it'll be right difficult, Tom. Anyway – the strike's official now.'

'And Jason *went* to work?'

She nodded. 'But he won't stick it, Tom. He thinks your dad's in the wrong.'

'I know. I heard.' Tom rose. 'Shall I take Linda to school for you?'

His sister's primary school was at the opposite end of the village to the Ernest Bevin Comprehensive, and normally Mrs Farrell delivered her daughter, before returning to do her housework.

'Ay, love. Save me a walk,' she said wearily. Tom glanced at his watch, knowing that his offer would make him late for school. As he left the room, leaving his mother sitting at the table with an anxious expression on her face, he made his voice sound jolly and confident. 'Don't *worry* about it so much, Mum. It'll all be over in a couple of weeks, you'll see!'

*

It was so *thrilling*, Melanie thought – too excited to eat her cereal. They had all sat up until late, Dad, Mum, Darren and her, talking about the strike. For once there was no television: this seemed far more real and important than anything they might watch on the small screen. 'Only five voted against,' her father had said.

'They'll be sorry,' growled Darren.

'No, lad, they'll change their minds. They'll not work,' said Mr Wall, straightening his back proudly like an army captain who had just led his men to victory.

'Sounds as if you carried the lot of them with you,' said Mrs Wall.

'That he did,' said Darren with pride.

Melanie had said nothing. She wanted to tell them that she had heard it all, but felt afraid that she would be accused of sneaking around and eavesdropping. Anyway, it didn't matter now. They were all together, the four of them, ready for what her dad called 'the fight'. Melanie didn't quite know what 'the fight' would be. She just knew that she was behind her dad, just as her mum was – and that somewhere outside there were mysterious 'others' who were not. The men who managed the pit. The men who were in charge of the National Coal Board which owned all the coal in the country. The government. The Prime Minister.

All of them ... And Tom Farrell's dad. But she quickly moved her mind away from that thought.

This day and the next there was an air of excitement in the playground. It buzzed around from person to person, almost alive, this sense of thrill and anticipation. A *strike*. The boys flexed their muscles, as if the 'fight' was a physical one and they were going to land punches on anyone who disagreed. The girls chatted in corners about how their parents had talked and behaved, whether there had been quarrels – which, in many cases, there had. In class they had found it hard to concentrate; now they were free to talk loudly – repeating, mostly, what their fathers had been saying the night before.

'We'll show them.'

'They'll have to take notice of us now.'

'They'll not get away with trying to sell us down the river.'

'We'll take 'em on, all right.'

And so on.

Tom Farrell was quiet. One or two of the other boys gave him odd looks, but since Tom was popular – as well as being big and tough for his age – nobody said anything to him. Only Lofty Lennard, the one boy in 3C who was taller than Tom, dared to speak. He came up casually, and folded his arms. 'What d'you think of last night then, Farrell?'

'Good night on TV,' said Tom.

'That's not what I mean, dafthead.'

'Then what *do* you mean, Lennard?'

Tom met the other boy's eyes. For a few moments they stared at each other in silence, then Lofty shrugged and turned away. 'You'll get square eyes,' was all he said.

'Better mind you don't get black ones,' called Tom.

The bell rang. The pupils moved towards the doors in groups, and Tom found himself next to Melanie in the line outside the chemistry lab.

'All right, then?' he asked.

'All right.' Then she hesitated. 'Tom . . .?'

'What?'

'Do you . . . *mind* – about your dad?' she whispered.

'What about him?'

She felt embarrassed, sensed her cheeks growing pink. 'You know, Tom. I mean that he . . . well, the others, they called him a coward and that, didn't they?'

He looked down at her. 'So what? Listen, Mel, I reckon its not being a coward to stand up for what you believe. All on your own. Is it?'

Melanie hadn't thought of that, and felt somehow relieved. 'No . . . it's not really. Not when you think about it,' she said thoughtfully, turning to grin broadly at him.

Tom felt suddenly light-hearted. That dreadful weight had gone from his stomach and he knew that everything would be all right. Already he was feeling that he needed a friend, although he didn't fully understand why.

Conscious of all the people around them he began to move away. But at the last minute he paused, and, without stopping to think, asked her if he could walk her to the Youth Club on Friday.

'You passing my house, then?' Melanie asked, wishing her cheeks were not pink. She knew exactly where he lived, much nearer to the Youth Club than she did. Normally he would not pass her house.

'Aye, that's right,' he replied very casually.

'Oh, might as well, then,' she said airily, hoisting her bag on her shoulder as if nothing mattered in the world.

CHAPTER THREE

'I'm baby-sitting tonight at Auntie Angie's,' Melanie said at teatime, two days later. Her brother sprawled, reading the newspaper. Her father was waiting for news of the strike on television, her mother was finishing off the last of the apple crumble.

Darren shook the newspaper in irritation. 'She's not your real auntie,' he said.

Melanie was astonished. 'What is she, then?' she asked. Susan Wall looked flustered. 'Well, if Mick is my cousin, she's my cousin-in-law, so to you she's . . . oh, I don't know. Too complicated to work out.'

'I really like Uncle Mick,' said Melanie, not really listening.

Darren was frowning now. 'No problem with *him*. He'll be on duty all right. *They* wouldn't miss it, the police. All lined up there, plenty of 'em, come from all over too. Any excuse to beat up our lads doing their picket duty. Cops! They hate us!'

'Darren!' said Mrs Wall, with a warning note in her voice.

'Right *keen* Mick is, Mother,' said Darren sarcastically, folding his newspaper and laying it down on the table.

'Well, he's got his job to do,' said Susan.

'And *we* have too – that's if there's jobs at all. 'Course, *he'll* be all right, there'll always be a job for *him*. Always jobs for coppers!' His voice was bitter.

Melanie looked from one to the other. Darren was usually a happy-go-lucky seventeen year old, thinking only of the weekends, and girls, of course. Her mother was always ... her mother: sparkling and cheerful, whatever happened. Now Darren looked angry and Susan looked anxious, and Melanie had no idea why. Except – it was something to do with Uncle Mick. 'What's up with you tonight, Darren?' she asked.

'Now don't you start,' said Mrs Wall to her son, before he had a chance to open his mouth. 'I don't want you bringing Melanie ... into things.'

Darren rose quickly, pushing back his chair. 'You don't know what you're talking about, Mother. You can't keep people *out* of things, not now. We're all in it together.' And he left the room.

For a few minutes nobody said anything. Mrs Wall glanced at her husband, raising her eyes to the heavens as if asking for his support. But Jim Wall looked across the room at his wife, and shrugged. 'What d'you expect, love? The lad's right, anyway.' Then he turned keenly towards the TV screen.

Melanie watched the news, too. The leader of the National Union of Mineworkers was being interviewed, and then there was a film of striking men outside pits in different parts of the country, and noisy clashes of these pickets with lines of policemen. Her father muttered responses to what was being shown, occasionally slapping the arm of his chair if he disagreed.

News always used to bore her. As far as she was concerned this thing called 'politics' meant nothing, when they were closing wards in the hospital where her grandmother was a patient. All those politicians arguing with each other, and boasting about what they had done, and blaming the other side for everything that went wrong ... they were like the boys scrapping in the playground. But *now* – she knew it affected her whole life. That realization made Melanie feel grown-up – but weary, too. 'I'd better go – they're expecting me about now,' she said, getting up.

Her mother pulled her across to kiss her. 'Have a good time, love. And give little Rob a kiss from me. Tell Angie I'll come over and see her this weekend.'

The Goldings lived in one of the police houses, just behind the police station. Melanie loved their house: small and built of red-brick, with the windows and door arranged in a neat, even fashion, and a little square garden in front – like the pictures of houses small children draw. When she opened the square green wooden gate and walked up the path, she noticed how Mick's flowerbeds were crammed with daffodils and tulips in close rows, all still in bud, but with the promise of all the reds and yellows, pinks and oranges to come.

Angie Golding opened the door before Melanie had a chance to ring the bell. She was a small woman in her late twenties, who looked even tinier beside her husband. Tonight Melanie thought she looked as if she'd been crying.

'What's the matter?' she asked.

'Just your Uncle Mick. He's got to work tonight. Extra shift. So I'll have to go over to my mother's on my own. I'd not have gone, but my brother and his wife are going too, so . . .'

'Where's Rob?'

'In his cot already. He's still awake though, and I said you'd go up and see him.'

Melanie liked the warm smell in the toddler's room, a strange mixture of toys and talcum powder that reminded her of her own childhood. Or perhaps it was the clutter all around the room, teddies and plastic cars and bricks, and all the other things that secretly she would still like to be able to play with. Sometimes.

The two year old was jumping excitedly up and down in his cot. 'Men-alie! Men-alie!' he called.

She laughed, and picked him up. 'Oooh, you lucky little thing,' she whispered, kissing the little boy on his soft cheek. 'I wish I was you in that cot – that I do, Robbie. Now, it's time for bed . . .'

'No bed. No bed,' he said, pulling her hair. 'Men-alie play!'

It took some time before he let himself be put back under the quilt, with his toy dog and rabbit. Downstairs again, Melanie found Angie Golding in the hall, putting on her coat. 'Auntie Angie . . .?' she said.

'Yes, love?'

'You won't be back late?'

'No, love.'

'Will Uncle Mick be in at all?'

Angie frowned. 'Not very likely, pet, There's already been trouble at the pithead, and they need all the men they can get. You ask your Dad and Darren, Melanie. They're down there all the time, shouting and screaming. My Mick, he just has to stand there and take it. I mean to say, it's not his fault.'

'What isn't?'

'That he's got to do his job. He's just a policeman, and so he has to see that those that wants to work can go in without getting thumped. That's all, Just his job. Don't you understand, Melanie? My Mick's not the village bobby anymore. He's the Public Enemy Number One.'

Melanie was shocked by the hardness in Angie's voice. Uncle Mick a 'public enemy'? He was the policeman everyone knew, who coped with unruly boys with a quick cuff and a word to their dads, and was famous for his repertoire of silly jokes. 'Have you heard the one about . . .?' he would start, and the kids would groan, loving it. Mick Golding was *popular*. He was her chocolate policeman.

And indeed, Angie was holding something out to her – a silver and blue wrapped bar of chocolate. 'He left this for you, pet. Now. I've got to go, or I'll be late.'

'Mum said to say she'll be over on Saturday or Sunday for a cup of tea,' said Melanie.

For a second she thought Angie looked surprised, but then a warm smile lit up the young woman's face. 'Good – you tell her I'll be right glad to see her too,' she said, as she went out.

Later that night Tom Farrell sat in front of the television in their living room, listening to the voices that came through the thin walls from the kitchen. Angry voices. Voices raised to shout down the other, with his mother's low pleading sound in the middle.

He knew it would happen when Jason burst through the front door panting, his face dark with rage. Tom's brother was not tall, but he was strong and stocky, and when he was angry he lowered his head and looked like a bull about to charge.

Jason and Tom were like peas from different pods. The four year age gap between them need not have mattered, but with them it did. Jason had always treated him like a kid, even when Tom grew old enough to share his brother's tastes in pop music and television programmes. He knew that his brother was jealous because their parents made such a fuss about Tom being 'good at school'.

'Nothing wrong with the pit,' Jason would say, putting his elbows on the table to shovel down his food, even though he knew their mother hated him to behave that way at the table. 'No good being snobby and going about with your head stuck in a book. Not in *this* world – no way!'

Tom would never reply. What was the point of quarrelling? He didn't see why people wanted to be the same. Jason had always been clever with his hands and could make things with wood – lovely things, like the beautiful doll's fourposter bed he carved for Linda one Christmas, and the bookshelf he made for their mother. Tom could not do things like that. He could come top of the class in English and Geography, and usually Maths and History too – and that was what *he* was good at. Why should Jason mind?

He walked into the kitchen to see Jason and his father confronting each other like a pair of boxers. 'It's not right, Dad, and you know it,' Jason shouted.

Mr Farrell spoke more quietly now. 'Don't tell me what's right and what's not right,' he said. 'I've been in this world long enough to make up my own mind.'

'Been in this world so long you're too old to see sense!' said Jason.

'Don't speak to your father like that,' said Mrs Farrell.

'Why shouldn't I?' Jason retorted, 'when he's showing me up like this? Making me do the same as him. Turning me into some kind of chicken! Well, I'll not stand for it.'

'You'll do as you're told,' shouted Tony Farrell.

'You're a fool, that's what you are!' Jason yelled. 'You'll lose all your friends, and for what? Who cares about you? You'll end up with no job, and no friends, and nothing. All because you're too damn chicken to go on strike.'

'Don't *say* that to our dad, Jason.'

The older boy whirled round, and looked coldly at Tom. 'Don't poke your nose in! What're you standing staring at, anyway?'

'I'm not staring, Jason. It's a bit hard to go anywhere in the house without hearing you, so I thought I'd come in.'

'Cheeky kid.'

'I'm not a kid, Jason.'

For a few seconds the two brothers stared at each other coldly. Then Jason looked away. 'I can't stand being in this house,' he said in a voice that suddenly sounded more upset than angry. 'You're all against me.'

'*Then don't stay in it,*' shouted his father.

'Tony!' pleaded Mrs Farrell. 'Don't talk to the boy like that. You'll drive him away. He's your *son*. He's more important than . . .'

'It's all right, Mum, I'm going. I'm not staying here to be told what to do by *him*. I'm going to join my mates on the picket line.' And Jason rushed from the room, slamming the front door so hard that the little house shook.

Mr Farrell was a stocky man, like his elder son. Now he sat hunched at the table, his square jaw set, his fists clenched. A frown creased his forehead.

It frightened Tom. His father rarely raised his voice to his sons – and never to his little daughter. He gave them lectures from time to time about the value of hard work, and how the only way you get anywhere in the world is by pushing yourself to do better than the next man . . . and so on.

Jason never listened. Tom took it all in. His father practised what he preached. On Saturdays and Sundays he worked in the house, building things, wall-papering, helping his wife with the housework. And when he wasn't doing that he was cleaning out the pigeons, or reading his books on vintage cars – his passionate interest. He was a straight, fair man, with an even temper. Tom could not remember when he had seen him look as angry as now he did.

'Linda gets right upset when there's a shouting match,' Tom said at last.

'Ay, I know,' sighed Mr Farrell, the frown disappearing at the mention of his daughter's name. 'But it can't be helped. There'll be plenty more angry words before this is over.'

Tom's mother looked as if she was about to cry. 'But Tony, you can't tell our Jason what to do. He's too old now.'

'I can tell him if I think he's letting me down,' said her husband stubbornly.

'But he thinks ... he says ...' – Tom's mother hesitated – 'he thinks it's *you* who's letting *him* down.'

The frown came back. 'I know what's *right*.' His clenched fist hit the arm of the chair. 'Jason – he's just like the rest of 'em. Hotheaded. They think you can save the world by standing shouting on a picket line. Think that the government will hear you in London, and tell the Coal Board not to close your pit. Him and the rest – they don't see any further than the noses on their faces.'

'He says he won't follow you to work tomorrow,' said Mrs Farrell quietly.

'Let him strike, then – my own son, too. He'll soon get back to work when he's got no money to buy his beer!'

'Dad?' Tom said.

'Yes, son.'

'I think people are going to ... well, what I mean is, when they ask me ...' His voice tailed away.

Tony Farrell looked at his son with a strange expression.

'Come on, out with it!' he said.

'See, Dad, I want to be on your side. I am on your side. But if they ask me in school *why* you're still working, what do I tell 'em?'

His father rose and walked across the room towards Tom. Then he did something very unusual – he put an arm around Tom's shoulders and hugged him hard. It made Tom feel like a small boy again, and to his horror, he felt tears start in his eyes, as if squeezed out by his dad's affection.

'You tell them people have to do what they think is right, Tom. I've been a Union member all my working life, and I've been on strike when it was the right thing to do. But this time it's wrong. We can't win. If there's less call for coal now, we've got to drag ourselves into the twentieth century. We got to talk about the future, not the past. *I'm* not sacrificing *my* family because my Union leaders want to pick a fight with this government. It'll be summer soon ... What a time to call a coal strike, eh! It's a waste of time, just a wicked waste of time.'

He paused, and removed his arm from Tom's shoulders, looking at him full in the face.

'Do you understand, son?'

'Yes, Dad.'

'So if they ask you in school – will you tell 'em all that?'

'Ay ... but I reckon they won't listen.'

'It'll be hard for him, Tony,' said Mrs Farrell, looking anxious. 'The other lads might pick on him and that. You know how they get ...'

Tom stood up straight, and threw his shoulders back. He was already as big as his dad. 'I can look after myself, Mum, don't you worry,' he said.

It was nearly midnight when he heard Jason's key in the door, then the heavy footsteps on the stairs. Tom looked forward to the day Jason would leave home; then he would have the bedroom to himself.

He lay quietly, pretending to be asleep. Jason stumbled slightly as he opened the wardrobe door. Then his bed creaked as he sat down heavily. There was a long silence. Tom could hear his brother breathing in the darkness. It was as if Jason was waiting. At last he whispered, 'You asleep, Tom?'

'No.' Tom smiled to himself, relieved. Jason sounded better. Tom realized how much he wanted to be friends with his brother. Ever since he was a tiny boy he had looked up to the older boy, and even the frequent coolness between them now could not alter that. It would be all right. They would talk it through . . .

'Well, what did Dad say then? Call me a load of names, did he?' asked his brother, in a sour voice.

'No.'

'Reckon there's not much *to* say,' said Jason. 'I'm not working tomorrow, whatever happens. None of my mates is working, and I'm not standing out against them. Not for *him*.'

'He's your dad, Jason,' said Tom.

'Ay, more's the pity,' replied his brother bitterly.

'Don't say that.'

'Why not? It's true, isn't it? He's going to work when everyone's on strike, and if we don't stand together they'll beat us. He knows that. He's got no loyalty – it makes me *sick!*'

Tom bit his lip in the darkness. It was as if someone had started to run a film inside his mind. He saw them on holiday in Blackpool when Linda was a baby, all on the beach, playing french cricket, having a good time. Then Christmases when they'd have to wait until noon before opening their presents, and Dad would take Jason and him for a walk, to stop their impatience. There'd be days out in the hills, when their Dad would take them birdspotting – before Jason grew too old to bother with that sort of thing. Watching the football on TV, building Mum's kitchen units, going out to choose a new power drill . . . together. They were always together, and they didn't quarrel much – not like other families.

Until now. All the happy images faded, and were replaced by – nothing. Just this darkness, and the tight sound of Jason's voice, and the memory of the shouting downstairs. Tom sat up in bed, angry now. 'Don't talk like that, Jason,' he hissed. 'Don't you say our dad makes you sick!'

He heard his brother slump heavily into bed. When he spoke, his voice had a nasty ring to it Tom had never heard before, not even when they disagreed. 'Yeah, well, I wouldn't expect anything else of my little goody-goody brother, would I? You just mind your own business, and keep your mouth shut. You're just a stupid kid, and you don't know nothing. Okay? *Nothing!*'

CHAPTER FOUR

It was Friday evening at last. Melanie thought it had been one of the strangest weeks she had ever known. Not all bad either – just different. She felt all the time that something thrilling was about to happen – a feeling that was partly to do with the unusual atmosphere at home. It was like electricity in the air – crackling all round the table as they sat having their tea, and talking about the strike.

Susan Wall was passionately behind it. 'If you don't hold out now, they'll walk all over you,' she said again and again. Jim Wall looked at her proudly. 'Most of the wives think like you do, love,' he said.

'I know they do! We've been talking. We're going to form our own group in Mainthorpe, to do what we can to help. And some of us are going to come down to the picket lines, too.'

At that Melanie's father shook his head, smiling at her fondly. 'No, I don't think the picket's the place for women, pet.'

'That it's not, Mum,' Darren agreed. 'It can get quite rough, you know.'

'Ay,' said Mr Wall, looking meaningfully at Melanie. 'Our Melanie knows that now, don't you?' Melanie crimsoned and looked down.

It had happened that morning. Mrs Wall had left earlier than usual, in a rush. Melanie was about to leave for school when she saw the small plastic sandwich box lying on the draining board in the kitchen. It was her father's; he must have forgotten it. Melanie was delighted, and all thoughts of school flew from her head. Her father and brother had forbidden her to go anywhere near the pit and the picket line, but this was a perfect excuse. She would take her father his 'snap'; nobody could blame her for that.

It was a long walk to the colliery, but on Melanie's old bike the journey only took ten minutes, and as she bowled along she felt excited. She imagined a line of men, her father at the head, all clapping and cheering as she rode up. There would be a brazier; she could warm her hands . . .

Despite all she had heard, and seen on television, Melanie was not ready for the scene she confronted as she turned her bike down the short piece of wide road that led to the colliery gates. The noise had grown as she had approached, like the swelling roar of an angry, wounded creature. Now it was as if the quiet world she knew had suddenly erupted into a frenzy of screaming and chanting, of flailing arms and legs, and of faces contorted with fury. There was no sign of the orderly little picket line she had expected. The dark line of police, many of them without helmets, were pushing back a mass of men, all of whom were shouting abuse at four or five other men who were trying to walk through the crowd and up to the gates.

'SCAB! SCAB! SCAB!'

She recognized Tom Farrell's father. He was not walking proudly, as she might have imagined, but with bent shoulders – as if to ward off blows.

The expressions on both sides appalled her: ordinary Mainthorpe faces – some of which she knew – violently twisted into masks of hate. And yet some of the younger men looked excited too, linking arms, pushing with considerable strength, and singing, 'Here we go, here we go, here we go!'

Then it was the roar of fury again: 'SCAB! SCAB! SCAB!'

She was standing staring, when footsteps behind her made her whirl round. It was Mick Golding, his helmet off, his skin dead white, one cheek already showing a livid blue and yellow bruise. The face which Melanie only knew as jolly and good-looking in a rosy, round-faced way, had altered; there was panic and confusion in Mick's expression. 'Melanie! What the hell are you doing out here?' he gasped, taking hold of her arm with a grip that was not gentle.

'Ow, Uncle Mick! I just came to bring our dad his sandwiches. He forgot them, so I . . .'

'This is no place for kids. You should be in school, anyway. You'll catch it – and you deserve to, if you ask me. Now you just get out of here!'

And with that, Mick Golding rushed away, to take his place with the other policemen. Melanie was horrified; he had not smiled once; he was like a stranger. The horrible shouting and scuffling frightened her, and yet she was fascinated, and wanted to stay to see what happened. Wanted to listen to that noise which grated harshly on her ears. Wanted to be part of it, yet wanted to run away. Melanie did not know what to do.

And all the time: 'SCAB! SCAB! SCAB!'

It was Mr Wall who decided for her. He ran up, staring at her as if she were a ghost. Sweat ran down his forehead: one arm of his jacket was torn.

'There had better be a good reason for this, young lady,' he panted, standing by her with his hands on his hips.

Wordlessly, Melanie held out the sandwich box, feeling the tears well up in her eyes. It wasn't that she was afraid of getting into trouble; it was the noise, and those faces, and the harshness of Uncle Mick, and . . . everything. Mr Wall saw that she was upset, and packed her off with few words. When she arrived at school they were halfway through the first lesson – French. Melanie had to stay in at break to make up the work.

In a way, she was astonished she could think of anything as normal as Youth Club, after what she had seen that morning. But life must go on, as her Gran always said. So she went upstairs to get ready. Fred, her old teddy, was sitting on her pillow. She picked him up and buried her nose in his fur. He smelt wonderful – as if years and years of hugging had impregnated his funny ancient fat body with a loving scent that would immediately comfort her. As it did now. 'Oh Fred the Ted,' she whispered, 'sometimes I wish I was a little girl again, and it was just me and you, playing games. Life's so *difficult*. This morning . . . oh Fred, they all *hate* each other so much.'

She stood for a few moments, brooding on what she had seen. But Melanie could not be downhearted for long, and she had something to look forward to. Soon she was rummaging in her wardrobe, choosing what to wear. Skirts joined jeans and jumpers in a pile on the bed, shoes and boots lay on the floor, as Melanie struggled with the problem. She looked at her watch. Fifteen minutes to go. Melanie found she was nervous, as if she had to stand up in front of the class and make a speech or something. Quickly she pulled her blue jeans, and the big pink sweatshirt trimmed with glittering studs, from the pile on the bed. White lace-up basketball boots . . . that would do. She sang along with the radio, and did not hear the doorbell ring.

A little earlier, about half a mile away, the Farrell family had reached crisis-point. Jason was leaving. Tom sat helplessly on his bed, dressed in his best jeans for Youth Club, as his brother rampaged around the small bedroom, stuffing clothes into a sports bag.

'Don't go, Jase,' he said miserably.

'I'm going,' his brother snapped.

'What's the point? You'll only upset Mum.'

'That's up to her. She's siding with *him*. She can choose, can't she?'

'But you can't ask her to choose between Dad and you – he's her husband, you're her son. She can't do that!'

'Everybody's got to pick their sides in this. It's not my fault,' said Jason in a quieter tone.

'Yes, and it's not Dad's fault, either. I think families should stick together, whatever happens,' said Tom.

'Do you, then? Well, I don't. I don't care about his stupid principles, and I don't care much about the damn strike either! But I'm not going against my mates, and the whole village! And I'm not staying in this house anymore.'

With that he marched from the room. Mrs Farrell was hovering on the landing. 'Where are you going to stay?' she cried, trying to hold his arm.

Jason pulled himself away. 'I'll sleep on Pete's floor,' he shouted over his shoulder. Pete Douglas was the brother of Tom's best friend Lee; another brother, Robert, was in the fifth form at the Ernest Bevin. The three Douglas boys lived with their father in a small house very near the mine. Their mother had left home when they were quite small, and although Tom found such a thought terrible, the friendly chaos of the little Douglas house appealed to him. His own mother was always cleaning, even when the place was spotless, and then complained a lot about all the work she had to do.

'But you haven't had any tea . . .' she wailed, at her elder son's departing back.

Tom followed his mother downstairs. When the

door slammed behind Jason, Mrs Farrell walked slowly into the sitting room, looking miserable.

'Well, at least I'll have my room to myself,' said Tom, trying to sound cheerful. No one said anything. Then Linda, who had been sitting in front of the television with her father, burst into tears and ran upstairs.

Mrs Farrell looked angrily across the room at her husband. 'Well, are you satisfied now, Tony?' she asked.

Tom's father sighed. 'So you think it's my fault, Elaine?' he asked, in a voice that was not angry, but sad.

She looked at the floor, and hesitated. 'Well, not really. But now our Jason's gone, and people are giving us funny looks in the streets, and . . . oh, I don't know, Tony . . .'

'What don't you know?'

'Whether . . . well, if it's any good trying to stand out against the crowd.'

'Do you think I should go on strike, love?' her husband asked quietly.

'No, I don't. But . . .'

He sat down heavily. 'If you don't take my side I don't know who will,' he said, in that same sad voice.

Tom couldn't bear it. '*I'm* on your side, Dad,' he said.

He remembered that as he turned into Melanie's street. His father had looked at him with a quick grin of gratitude, and suggested they both go out to check the pigeons. In that warm fluttering darkness they were happy and close. Just as it always used to be. Tom knew that the memory would take him through lots of cool stares in the street. And at school – even from Eddy and Lee . . .

He rang the door bell, looking at his watch. He was early. She probably wouldn't be ready. Jason always said that girls took ages to get ready. Tom smiled, feeling suddenly shy. This was the first time he had ever called for a girl, and it felt strange. But Melanie had given him special friendly looks in school, even though they had not spoken much. He needed that feeling of friendship. He was looking forward to seeing her.

The light went on in the hall, and the door opened. Darren Wall stood there, a mug of tea in his rough miner's hand, and a welcoming look on his face. But when he saw Tom his expression changed in a second, becoming closed-off and cool.

'What?' he said.

'Um, I've er . . . I'm walking Mel down to Youth Club.'

'You what?'

'Didn't she say anything about it? I told her I'd be here, but I'm a bit early.' Tom felt puzzled.

'You're too early, right enough.' Darren's voice was cold.

Tom began to understand. It was as if someone started to pull open a curtain in his mind, throwing light on something he did not want to see or know – something horrible. He looked at the ground, shuffling his feet. 'Well, I reckon I'll walk up and down the street and come back a bit later then,' he said awkwardly.

'Don't bother coming back at all,' Darren said in a rough voice, starting to close the door. But before he could, Susan Wall appeared in the hall behind him.

'Who is it, love . . . oh!' She saw Tom, and looked at him oddly for a second. Then she smiled, but awkwardly. 'It's Tom Farrell. So *you're* the lad who's coming to walk Melanie to Club!'

'Ay,' Tom said shyly.

'I've told him to go and not come back, Mother,' said Darren.

Susan looked from Tom to Darren and back again.

'Now, Darren,' she said firmly, 'it's none of your business who Mel wants to be friends with. All right? It's got nothing to do with you.'

Darren turned and handed her his mug, as if he wanted his hands free. 'She's *my* sister,' he said firmly, jabbing a thumb in his own chest.

As if she heard, Melanie chose that moment to come pounding down the stairs, looking self-conscious. 'Oh . . . you're early, Tom Farrell,' she said airily. 'I'll just get my jacket.'

'No, you won't Melanie!' said Darren furiously.

'What's up?' she asked with astonishment.

Don't say it, don't say it, thought Tom. He stared at Darren, willing him to stay quiet, to go away, to leave them alone. But the young miner stood facing him, looking at him with – yes – *contempt* in his eyes.

'I'm not having my sister walking down the street with a . . . with a . . .'

Don't say it, don't say it . . .

'What are you talking about Darren?' Melanie asked, in a pleading voice.

'I'm not having *my* sister seen with a *scab*,' her brother said, glaring at Tom as if he despised him utterly.

That word. The ugly name they shouted at the men who went to work when the rest were on strike. The name that was screamed each day at his own father. But what had it to do with him? Nothing. And yet he had known it would be thrown at him, he had known it in his dreams.

Melanie was speechless. It was Mrs Wall who broke the silence. 'Now you listen to me, Darren. It doesn't help anyone, or anything, to go round calling people names. It's Tom's father who's a . . . er . . . who's working. It's not Tom. It's got nothing to do with Tom. It's not his fault his dad's . . .'

For a second Tom wanted to agree with her. He

wanted to say that his father had nothing to do with him. But then he knew that he couldn't betray him like that. Not his own father. It *was* something to do with him.

'It's not my fault, Mrs Wall, but I'm not ashamed of my dad,' he said, standing up straight, and looking at Darren as he spoke.

'See?' Darren said.

Melanie was furious now. 'You just mind your own business, Darren Wall. You can't pick my friends, and you don't call my friends names, either!'

'All right, then,' replied her brother. 'I'll just go indoors and fetch our dad, and see what he has to say about you walking down the street in front of the whole village, with a *scab's little boy*.' There was such hatred in those last words that Tom felt his blood chill.

'Don't bother,' he said proudly, stepping back from the doorstep. 'I reckon I'll go.' And without another word he turned sharply, and walked quickly away down the street.

When he turned the corner, Tom stopped and leaned against the wall, panting. His knees felt weak. He could feel the blood hot in his face, and realized – when he unclenched his fists – that his nails had been digging painfully into the palms of his hands. *It wasn't fair*, he thought angrily. *It just was not fair*.

He shifted his weight, and rested his burning cheek against the rough, cold brick. It felt comforting. For some reason it reminded him of something in his childhood – of resting his face against his father's old scratchy tweed jacket, when they would go out for long walks and Tom would grow tired, so his father would carry him. Half falling asleep, and the bumpiness of his dad's strides, and the feel of that rough material rubbing against his face and smelling of . . .

of Dad. And all the time the knowledge that at home the fire would be lit, and Mum would have a hot water bottle ready in his bed, and the old felt dog would be waiting there, rough and dear and familiar like his dad's coat.

All gone, those safe times. That jacket had gone for jumble years ago, and the little dog had come apart at the seams, so that his mother had thrown it out and made him cry. How old was he then ... seven? And now he was leaning against a wall in the street, feeling that the world hated him and it was not his fault.

He heard the sound of running feet, and tensed. Without knowing what he was doing, he made his hands into fists once more. Then he began to stride quickly along, without looking behind him.

'Tom! Tom!'

It was Melanie's voice. But still he did not look round or stop.

'Tom! *Wait* for me!'

At last she caught up with him, and pulled on his arm, panting. He had to stop, and faced her.

'I'm sorry, Melanie,' he said formally, as if they had only just met and he had jogged her arm or something.

'What do you mean, *you're* sorry?' she panted. 'It's not you that should be sorry, Tom. Ooooh, I've never been so mad in all my life, I haven't!'

She stamped her foot. Tom shrugged. 'Well, I don't suppose you should be seen with me, Mel. Not if Darren says.'

'What's it got to do with him? Do you think I do everything my brother says? You must think I'm a baby, Tom Farrell!'

When Tom said nothing, she nudged him in the ribs. 'Oh, *come on!*' she said irritably, and set off down the road. Tom had no choice but to walk beside her. But he dreaded Darren coming behind them – not because he was afraid of the older boy (Tom flexed his arm muscles proudly; he wasn't afraid of anyone) but in case he got Melanie into trouble. Mind you, he thought, glancing down at her, Melanie could probably look after herself. She had her hands thrust in her pockets, and her curly head thrown back, and an extremely determined set to her jaw, as if she wouldn't take any nonsense from *anybody*. He liked that. He liked tomboys.

'None of his *b* . . . business,' she muttered. Tom grinned at the swear word she had not said.

'That's right, Mel,' he said, feeling happier.

'Darren – he's always treating me like a little kid,' she said. 'But he's okay, really. I mean, he's always been good to me – giving me money, and that.'

'Jason's left home,' Tom said.

'Why?'

Tom shrugged. 'What do you think? He and my dad were arguing all the time, and Jason went back to work, and then he said he couldn't stand to be in the same house as Dad. Said that Dad's a . . . you know.' He couldn't bring himself to say the word.

Melanie just nodded. 'I know,' she said.

They reached 'The Rave Cave', and stopped automatically to look in the window. Melanie said gloomily, 'There's no money for stuff like that. Not now. There's no strike pay, is there?'

Tom felt awkward. 'Reckon not.'

'Does you dad go on getting paid? I suppose he must.'

'Yeah, and I reckon he deserves it for walking through that lot every day,' said Tom with grim defiance.

There was a short silence. Melanie looked at Tom sideways, thinking suddenly that it wasn't fair. Not life itself – she was already getting used to the idea that, as her mother often said, life is never fair. But this in particular – that Tom's dad should go on working and get paid, whilst her dad did not. Then she drove the thought away. That was how it was. That was the mess they were in. 'Oh, come on, let's go,' she said.

The youth club was held each Friday in the church hall, down a back street in Mainthorpe. It was an old building of blackened brick, with small high windows, making it look rather like a small prison. As Tom and Melanie approached they heard loud music.

'Melanie!' someone shouted.

They both stopped and turned round. Jackie was walking up the road with Lofty Lennard and his two friends, Billy Yates and Dave Mugford.

'Oh, no,' Melanie whispered. Tom drove his hands even deeper into his pockets and hunched his shoulders.

The group drew close to them. Jackie was pink, and nudged Melanie sharply in the ribs, saying, 'Hey up, then Mel! Who keeps her secrets, then?'

Lofty swaggered close by her, possessively. He looked mockingly at Melanie and Tom, and said, 'Does your mother know you're out, Wallsie?'

'I don't know what you're talking about,' Melanie replied.

'I mean – does she know who you're *with*?' he said, in a jeering voice.

Melanie glanced at Tom, wanting him to speak. But he just stood there, looking at the ground. She knew that would drive Lofty on. She could feel her face growing red, and was glad that it was dark. ''Course my mum knows,' she retorted, 'and it's none of your business anyway, Lennard.'

The other boys made silly noises, backing away from her as if afraid. 'Watch it, Lofty, she might bite,' said Dave.

'Oh, don't be so daft,' said Jackie, taking Melanie's arm. 'Come on then, Mel, you walk along with me.'

Melanie hesitated, looking at Tom, who still said nothing. Lofty was staring at him aggressively. 'What's the matter, Farrell?' he said at last. 'Too scared to speak?'

Tom looked at him calmly for a few seconds. Then he said, 'I'm not scared of anything,' in a quiet voice.

'Scared of walking into Club with your girlfriend, I reckon,' Lofty said, breaking into a raucous laugh. 'Or I reckons it's her who's scared. Melanie *Wall* don't want to be seen out with a scab, do you, lass? Not with your dad at the front line over there . . .' And he jerked a thumb in the direction of the pit, laughing even more loudly.

'Come on, Mel. Leave the lads to fight it out,' Jackie said, pulling her arm once more.

'I'm doing no fighting,' said Tom in that same calm, quiet voice, ignoring the others and looking straight at her. 'So are you going to walk along the rest of the way with me, Mel?'

Melanie hesitated. Jackie's arm felt familiar and safe. Tom stood alone in the middle of the pavement, his face pale in the gloom. People would see them together; people would say things, people would say *that* . . .

'I'll just walk in with Jackie, Tom,' she said awkwardly, trying to smile at him, 'and I'll see you inside, all right?'

'All right,' he said.

When the girls had turned up the path Tom jingled the money in his pocket. It was fifty pence to get into the club, and he had taken two pounds out of his money box, enough to pay for both of them and to buy her a bottle of cola too, and maybe a chocolate bar. His hand chased the coins around his pocket, then closed on them all, tightly. He gripped them so hard they dug into his flesh, hurting him. But nothing could hurt as much as the disappointment, like an ache in his chest.

Oh, what's the point, he thought, wanting to go home. He thought of his room, peaceful now that Jason had gone, and longed to turn and run home as fast as he could, replace the money in his box, and hide from the world. He would check the pigeons, then lie on his bed and strum his guitar, and forget about it all . . .

The noise of pop music filled the street, sounding horrible and discordant to him now. But he had to see it through, he knew he did. 'I don't care what happens to me,' he said to himself. 'I'll show them I'm not scared. Just like my dad's not scared.'

And so Tom Farrell took his hands out of his pockets, stood straight, and walked nonchalantly up to the door of the youth club.

CHAPTER FIVE

It was dark and noisy inside. Groups of boys stood
together, and girls danced together, as they always
did. At one end of the hall there was a bright square of
light, in which the youth worker, Mary Roberts, was
framed, standing in her small 'shop' selling canned
drinks and chocolate bars and hot dogs to the Mainthorpe youth. Near this haven was an old snooker
table, and an equally rickety table tennis table, both
surrounded by boys who watched the games being
played with quiet concentration, broken only by occa-
sional cries of encouragement.

'Hello, Tom, how's it going?' Mary Roberts's husband Colin was the other youth leader, and he slapped
Tom on the shoulder in his normal way.

'All right,' said Tom.

It was all as usual. Everything the same: the music,
the kids, the slightly musty smell, Colin Roberts's
ginger beard and his broad grin, the sudden sounds of
argument from the ping pong table . . . all looked as it
normally did.

So what was different? Tom felt puzzled. The youth
leader was looking at him strangely.

'What's up, lad? You've a queer look on your face.'

'Have I?'

'Ay – you look like you've lost a pound and found 10p. What is it – girl trouble?'

'Don't be daft,' said Tom, looking away.

Down the hall he saw Melanie dancing with Jackie and two other girls, all bobbing around in a world of their own. Yet they were all together – they looked as if they belonged together. So did the boys around the games tables. And the crowds leaning by the shop. All *together*.

'That's what's different,' thought Tom. 'It's me. *I'm* different.' Something was happening to him – but what?

At that moment Lee Douglas sauntered in through the door near where they stood.

'Hey up!' said Tom.

For a moment he thought he saw a look of worry – and of *evasion* – in his friend's eyes. But he must have been imagining it, because Lee stopped. They stood in silence for a minute or two, but that was not unusual.

The silence continued. Then Lee shuffled his feet. 'Er . . . look, I'm going down to play table tennis. See you,' he muttered, and strode quickly down the hall.

Melanie had seen Tom come in. She felt embarrassed and disappointed at the same time. If only they hadn't met the others . . . But in any case, the evening had been spoiled from the beginning. Darren had spoilt it. Meeting Jackie and the others, and her choosing to go in with Jackie . . . it just carried on what Darren had started.

Suddenly tired of dancing she moved to the side of the hall, and flopped down on a chair. Jackie joined her. 'You look nice tonight, Mel,' she said, panting slightly.

Melanie pulled irritably at her own sweatshirt. 'Shouldn't have worn this thing. I'm too hot,' she snapped.

A girl from their class walked up to stand in front of

them, and Jackie looked at her, winking. 'Don't speak to Mel, Lindsay, or you'll get your head bit off. Nothing's right with her tonight, is it, Mel?'

But Melanie took no notice. She was staring with a fixed expression at Tom Farrell, who was strolling down the middle of the hall, sidestepping the dancers. He made his way to the little 'shop', jingling the coins in his pocket.

Tom was aware that two boys had been waiting to be served as well, but moved abruptly away as he approached. He thought little of it; they had probably changed their minds about spending their money. Then someone said loudly, just behind him: 'Here comes Farrell, the one with the money. When your dad's a scab you can afford things.'

Tom recognized the voice but did not turn round. He swigged deeply from his canned drink, as if it were a hot summer day and he had no cares.

'Chicken!' Lofty hissed in his ear. There was such contempt in the word that Tom felt a wave of anger sweep over him – choking and blinding. He was about to swing round when Mary Roberts laid both hands over his, as they rested on the bar.

'Now, Tom, *don't!*' she said in a low, firm voice. Then she raised it. 'Colin!' she called.

When Lofty had been quietly ejected from the building, so that few of the kids even noticed what had happened, Tom turned, leaning his back on the bar to face the room.

Melanie was still watching him, and he saw. Shyly he raised a hand to wave to her, and she smiled and nodded back. But she did not come over. It would have surprised him if she had. Even when a Mainthorpe boy walked a girl to the youth club, he rarely stayed with her once inside. They might dance slowly together towards the end of the evening, and he would certainly walk her home, but in general the boys and girls kept to their separate groups, like flocks of different birds.

And there would be no other reason for her to stay away from him, would there? *Would there?* Tom gave himself a mental shake. Of course there wouldn't.

He sauntered over to the ping pong table, standing behind the group of boys who were watching Lee and Eddy play a fierce match. Normally he would have shouted out immediately, teasing one or other of his friends to put him off his stroke. But tonight he was silent, conscious only of this sick feeling of dread in his stomach.

The table tennis ball spun off the table and passed through the legs of the boys in front of Tom. It clicked sharply against his foot, and he bent down to pick it up. 'Hey, Eddy, you're playing like my granny,' he called, aiming and tossing the ball high in the air, so that it dipped to hit Eddy, with beautiful precision, on the head.

The boys in front of him looked round. Most of them were older than Tom, boys from the fourth and fifth year at school, although at least two were in his own class. They had been talking and laughing, but when they saw Tom the cheerful hubbub ceased, as if it had been turned off. Most of the boys dropped their gaze and looked awkwardly away. Others stared at him with open hostility.

'Look who's here,' said a voice.

'Don't need to *look*,' said somebody else, sniffing at the air like a dog. There was some laughter, but it sounded nervous. Tom Farrell had always been popular, despite being good at school work, and so a few boys quickly moved away from the small group – unwilling to take his part, yet equally unwilling to bait him.

The boys parted as Tom moved forward. Eddy and Lee were standing by the ping pong table, looking at him. Tom held out his hand to Eddy.

'Here, give me that. I'll thrash him for you.'

Without looking at him, Eddy held out the old bat and mumbled, 'You do that.' Lee just stared at him, saying nothing, a slight flush of embarrassment in his cheeks.

Tom could hardly bear it. His friends. These were his best friends and they were behaving as if he were a stranger. It hurt, terribly. But he would never let them know how he felt.

So he grinned at Lee, and said in a challenging voice, 'Come on then, are you going to give me a game?'

Before Lee could reply a voice called, 'Don't play with him, Douglas!' Another took up the refrain, 'You wouldn't play with one of *those*, Douglas.'

Don't say it, please don't say it, don't say the word, pleaded Tom in his mind, desperate now. He felt as if his own life depended on the next few seconds.

'You've got a cheek showing your face in here, Farrell,' said one of the toughest fifth year boys.

Tom held his breath. He was still holding out the bat to Lee, and staring at his friend. Eddy stood nearby, and it was as if they were all frozen there, waiting. It seemed like half an hour or more, as the bat trembled slightly in his hand.

'Lee?' he said in a low voice, questioning.

Eddy was looking at him now, and Tom saw his gaze move from him to Lee and back again. At last he spoke. 'Go on, Lee, give him a game. I want a bit of revenge.'

Lee's cheeks were scarlet now. He opened his mouth to speak, his hands firmly clamped at his side. *He's going to say No; he won't play with me,* thought Tom.

But at that moment the older boy spoke again, in a loud, jeering voice. 'You don't want to play with a little *scab*, Douglas. Tell him where to stuff that bat.' And more than one voice took up the refrain, 'Little scab, little scab.'

Lee Douglas, a short tough boy with razored hair, did *not* like being told what to do. So at that, he reached forward and snatched the bat from Tom's hand. Glaring fiercely at the others he said, 'I'll play with who I like, okay?'

Tom relaxed a bit, and stared challengingly at the crowd. Eddy moved up to stand beside him now, turning to face the others. 'And the next one to call names will get this ball shoved down his throat,' he said, holding it aloft between his finger and thumb.

'Wait till your brother hears about this, Douglas,' the older boy muttered, in a nasty voice.

Tom winced. Jason was staying with Pete Douglas, and even though he didn't get on with his brother, his pride hated the idea of Jason knowing about scenes like this one. It would just turn him even more against Dad.

'Be best if everybody minded their own business,' he said angrily.

'Who asked you, little . . .' But Eddy and Lee stood beside Tom, and all three of them faced the others, and so the insult was not repeated.

'Oh, come on, let's play,' said Lee, and took his place at the end of the table.

The last thing Tom felt like doing was playing table tennis. But once the game had begun, all his pent-up anger and frustration was directed at that ball, so that Lee could hardly see the shots. Both boys were fast and skilful players but there was no doubt who had the upper hand. Tom served hard, and smashed at the ball, and spun it, thinking each time he drew back his bat that he was about to hit one of the people who had called him that name. Or those who shouted it at his father each morning when he went to the mine.

Eddy stood at the side watching, his face trying to show interest. But he looked miserable. So did Lee – who was playing like a robot, without his normal catcalls and whoops of glee. The space around the table was completely empty; nobody watched them.

Nobody that is – except Melanie. She stayed sitting in her corner, but stared fixedly at the table tennis game in the distance, until Jackie noticed.

'Ooh, Mel, I wish you'd stop,' she said.

'Stop what?'

'Looking at *them*. You'll get yourself into trouble,' Jackie whispered, with a meaningful look sideways.

'*Now* what are you on about?'

'I'm on about Tom Farrell.'

'What about him?.'

'Oh, his dad working and all.'

'What's that got to do with him?' Melanie asked in-dignantly.

'Oh, I don't know. I think it's all boring. But Lofty and his mates, they're going to send him to Coventry. Not speak to him in school, and that. And Lofty says anyone who's friends with Tom 'ull get the same treatment. Lofty told me . . .'

'Oh, Lofty, Lofty, Lofty, who cares what that great lout thinks?' snapped Melanie, furious now.

Jackie sniffed, tossing her hair. 'Well, I do, for one. I wouldn't want to go to school and nobody talk to me all day. It'd be right boring.'

'Right *mean!*' said Melanie. 'Listen, Jackie Meadows, are you saying that if I speak to Tom Farrell nobody'll speak to me? What about you? Wouldn't you speak to me?'

She got up and stood squarely in front of her friend. Jackie dropped her eyes, ashamed.

'Er yes, Mel . . . but . . .'

'But what?'

'Oh, nothing. But you just . . . just be careful, that's all. The lads get right mad. Everybody's mad. My dad, he goes on about it all the time.'

'So does mine,' said Melanie glumly, sitting down

again. 'I thought it was all exciting, till tonight. Now it's . . . it spoils things, sort of.'

'But you were going on yourself. You were saying how your mum's keen, and you're behind your dad all the way. Right?'

'Yes, but . . .' Melanie sighed.

If she had looked up she would have noticed a slight gleam of triumph in Jackie's eye, as she shrugged. 'Well, I'm not the world's greatest genius, Melanie Wall, but I know one thing. If you're on your dad's side, you can't stick up for Tom Farrell, too. You can't be on two sides at once, so there!'

Melanie said nothing. Was it true? She could see that it might be – and the thought was awful. The boys had been saying horrible things to Tom by the table tennis table, and now they had all moved away in that awful, obvious way, so that Tom, Eddy and Lee were left alone.

Taking a deep breath, she stood up. Jackie looked up at her. 'Where are you off to, Mel?' she asked.

'Home. I've had enough.'

'Already? They'll be serving the pies soon.'

'I don't want anything to eat. I'm off. See you, Jackie.'

Melanie did not turn towards the entrance. Instead she walked over to the table tennis table, where Tom and Lee were just finishing their second game.

At last Tom drew back his bat and smashed the ball across and down the extreme left hand side of the table. Lee lunged, but had no chance of returning it. He groaned, and threw down his bat.

'That's it,' he puffed.

'What about another game?' asked Tom. Lee shook his head.

'Play with *her*,' he said, jerking his head in Melanie's direction. Eddy nodded to him and laughed, but there was nothing unfriendly in the laughter. The boys liked Melanie, and she knew it.

The four of them stood awkwardly in silence for a moment. Melanie was aware of glances from elsewhere in the room, curious looks and nudges that made it seem as if she, Tom, Lee and Eddy were on a small island, surrounded by dangerous waters.

Then Lee said that he was going to get himself something to drink, and both boys moved away – walking in a selfconsciously slow way, like . . . cowboys in a western, Melanie thought.

Tom was fiddling with the binding around the bat handle, not looking at her.

'I thought I'd go home now,' said Melanie.

He jerked his head up, surprised. 'It's early,' he said.

'I'm fed up.'

'So am I.'

Tom looked at Melanie. 'You want me to walk you home then, Mel?'

But Melanie could feel the looks. She knew that most people in that room were staring at her, wondering what was going on. She couldn't bear it, and so she said nothing.

'So are you coming or not?'

She shook her head. 'No.'

'So you're going to stay?'

To her horror, Melanie could feel tears starting to well in her eyes. She looked steadfastly at the floor. 'No . . . er, I mean . . . I mean I'm going to go now, because I don't like it tonight. But you stay, Tom.'

'What you mean is, you don't want to be seen walking out with me,' he said flatly.

'No, it's not that . . .' she said helplessly, in a quavery voice.

'Yes, it is, Mel. I know,' he said quietly. 'Well, don't worry. I'm going now myself, so you won't have to be seen even talking to me. All right?' And with that Tom turned quickly, and strode down the hall, pushing his way through the kids who were drifting down towards the shop.

Melanie's cheeks blazed. But she ducked her head, picked up the bat, and pretended to be very interested in mending the binding that was becoming unravelled on the handle. Then she put it down carelessly, and strolled back to Jackie and the other girls, agreeing with them that it would be nice to share a pie.

When Tom closed the door of his bedroom behind him he felt safe at last. Yet why *safe*? All the way home he had been tempted to glance behind him. Yet the streets of Mainthorpe were empty. He knew that the pubs would be full, and that in most of the houses the television would be on. Nobody saw him, still less stepped out of the shadows to stop him and call him names, as he had feared.

He threw his jacket on Jason's bed, and flung himself full length on his own. His hands clasped behind his head, he stared at the ceiling, following the pattern of cracks and blemishes with his eyes, as if he would find solutions in its complicated twists and turns. But there were no solutions, he thought, just a mess.

It was a long time before he got up again, moving restlessly to the little table he used for his homework. Absent-mindedly Tom riffled through the untidy pile of papers and books, until he saw the essay competition entry form, slightly crumpled beneath his English text book. Funny old Skinny, thinking he should enter . . .

He picked it up, and read it again. 'Write on any subject you like, under the general heading "Freedom". It could be a story about animals in the zoo, or an essay about history, or an account of something that happened to you. What matters is that it should be well-written and all your own work.'

Tom threw it down. Huh, *freedom* – that was a good one. How could you be free when everybody expected you to act and think the same way as them? Freedom didn't exist, not in *his* world. Not now.

Thoughtfully he sat down at the table, pushing the papers aside with his arm to make a space. He took his pad of file paper and a felt tip pen, and sat chewing the end of it and staring at the curtains. Then, after a few minutes, he bent his head and began to write.

CHAPTER SIX

The next long weeks saw changes in Mainthorpe nobody could have imagined. The strike was like a huge octopus that snaked its tentacles around everyone and everything.

The Farrell family was not the only one split by quarrels. Attitudes hardened – and so did divisions. Now two brothers would pass each other in the street without speaking, because they were on different sides, and cousins were not allowed to play together because their parents involved them in a disagreement the small children knew nothing about. The strike started to squeeze the little community, and it hurt. People took refuge in their hatreds then, knowing who the enemy was.

The schoolchildren who had been excited about the strike were less happy when they realized just how poor their families had become. There was no pocket money now, and no extra treats. And fathers and brothers became bored and bad tempered, as they sat at home off picket duty. There would be no holidays this year. Family savings were used up, in the effort just to live, day to day.

Mothers did long sums on the backs of old envelopes, calculating how far the family allowance and family income supplement would stretch; and they travelled miles to jumble sales, in search of good second-hand clothing. Most of them were tough-minded, because they believed the strike was right. But some of them quickly grew weary and irritable with the penny-pinching.

It was the last day of the Easter holidays. Some chocolate eggs still stood on the shelf, unsold. It was the same in the supermarket and the newsagents: little stacks of Easter eggs, offered now at cut prices. Parents who would usually buy an Easter egg each for their children now gave them one to share. The small bakery where Mrs Wall worked did a poor trade in cakes. Bread sold, of course, for people must have bread. But cakes were a luxury and when times are hard, luxuries have to go.

Or so Susan Wall kept telling Melanie. For like all her friends Melanie began to complain about the lack of roast meat on Sunday, and the general atmosphere of need.

'Funny, isn't it,' sighed Jackie, as she and Melanie stared longingly at the clothes at 'sale' prices in 'The Rave Cave' window, 'how you sort of take things for granted. I used to think your mum and dad spoiled you a bit, Mel, much more than mine. But now I think *I* used to be rich, compared to now.'

'What did you get for your birthday?' asked Melanie vaguely.

'Not much. Just a bit of make-up, but it's nice. Some blue and green eyeshadow in a little box and a lipstick – pale pink. Mum's given me an old compact of hers, too.'

'My mum won't let me wear make-up,' Melanie said.

'Why?'

'Says I'm too young. And . . .' Melanie paused. This was the strangest thing of all, and she hesitated to talk about it.

'What?'

'She says it's a waste of time. She's sort of ... different, now, Jackie. She used to wear a lot of make-up herself, but she doesn't bother any more. It's funny, really.'

'What does your dad say?'

Melanie shrugged. 'Not much.'

That wasn't true. Her dad had a lot to say. More and more. At first he was glad that Melanie's mother was right behind him, as he said. But just lately his tone had changed. 'I want you behind me, but not in front of me, lass,' he had said firmly a few days ago.

Mrs Wall and a group of other women from Mainthorpe had started a Women's Support Group. There were groups like it all over the country – miners' wives and mothers gathering together and saying that they supported the strike and were going to do what they could to help. The older women were content to plan fund-raising events; the younger women, like Melanie's mother, didn't see why they shouldn't be involved in real action, too.

'The picket line's no place for women,' Jim Wall had told her, as usual.

'Why not?' Mrs Wall retorted.

'Because it gets violent, that's why!'

'We can shout as loudly as you men.'

'Louder!' laughed Darren, putting his fingers in his ears.

His mother looked at him indignantly. 'Typical!' she said crossly. 'You expect me to stay here and make your meals when there's no housekeeping money, and wash and iron your clothes as usual, and be strong enough to take all the ... all the ... *nastiness* that's around, yet you don't think I'm strong enough to go down to the picket line and shout my feelings out.'

Mr Wall tried a different tack. He smiled and pointed at the ground. 'Anyway, love, look at those shoes. You'd last five minutes tottering along in your red high heels!'

'Well then,' blazed his wife, whilst Melanie watched in astonishment, 'I'll not wear them. I'll not wear them ever again!' And she kicked the red shoes off her feet and under the table.

'Good for you, Mum!' said Melanie gleefully, while her father glowered at them both.

So Mrs Wall had won. The next morning she had gone into Melanie's room early, wearing no make-up and a determined expression. She had on jeans and trainers. 'Mel,' she said, pulling open the curtains as Melanie moaned and clutched Fred, hating the sudden light, 'get yourself up now, and get dressed and go down and start your own breakfast. I'm just popping down the road to have a word with Annie. We're going to work out rosters for the Women's Group to picket. I'll be back before you leave for school.'

Now, each day a small group of wives and mothers marched to the mine to join the men. Mrs Wall went every other day, usually after she had finished her part-time job. Sometimes she didn't return for a long time, and Melanie would let herself into the house and find a note asking her to peel some potatoes, put the pan on the stove on a low light, set the table or whatever. Often Darren would be there, sprawled in front of the television. 'Why can't you help?' she shouted at him once.

'That's women's work,' he said jokingly, as she carried in plates from the kitchen.

'You say that again, Darren Wall, and I'll drop these plates on your head. Knock some sense into it,' said Melanie grimly.

'It's already been knocked about enough by the police,' he said cheerfully, as if he were talking about a game they were all involved in, not something serious.

'Well, get up and help me, then!'

'No, it's all right, Mel, I'll let you practise for when you're married.'

'Ohhh, *you!*' She banged down the plates, grabbed a cushion and threw it at her brother. At that moment their father came through the door.

'Hey up! What's happening here?' he said.

'Mel's going berserk,' said Darren.

'He's being stupid, teasing me,' she said sulkily.

'Better clear that up before your mother comes in,' said Jim Wall, dropping into his armchair with a weary thud.

'Where is she anyway? At the pit?' asked Melanie, as she frantically dusted off the cushion cover.

Her father opened the newspaper, and gave it an indignant little shake. 'No, not today. Her and her friend Annie and the others, they're having a meeting in the hall. Some woman from London's come to talk to them. About the strike.'

'What d'they know about it down there?' Darren's voice was mocking.

'Nothing son, that's right. But some clever middle-class girl's come up to give our women a lesson in tactics. *Tactics!*'

'I wish they'd give our Darren a lesson in helping in the house,' muttered Melanie. 'I'll tell our mum what you said to me, Darren, you see!'

Her brother looked worried at the prospect. Though he was a man now, he still feared their mother's temper, her sharp words. So he made his voice wheedling: 'Don't do that, Mel. Don't tell on us!'

'Better get up off your backside and help her then,' said Mr Wall shortly. Darren raised his eyes to heaven, but heaved himself up and went to fetch the knives and forks. And Melanie felt she had won an important victory.

'You're getting more like your mother every day,' said her dad. His voice sounded as if he wasn't altogether glad.

60

People were changing in Mainthorpe. It was a slow process, not something you could easily put your finger on. The anger felt by the men who were on strike was easy to see. They would line up outside the pit, and shout at the handful of men who went to work. The Coal Board supplied a van with wire mesh over the windows to drive the working miners through the gates, because it became impossible for them to walk. When the women joined the men on the picket line the local policemen looked uncomfortable. They didn't mind pushing and jostling with men their own size, but with women . . .?

Melanie's 'uncle' Mick Golding shook his head at home, as Angie put a cup of tea in his hand.

'Y'see, we can't drag women about, love.'

'Well, they shouldn't be there, should they?' said Angie, angrily.

'Susan's there most days.'

'Well, you should have a word with her, Mick.'

'Don't be daft. What can I tell her? Better if you spoke to her – woman to woman, like.'

'She's *your* cousin,' Angie replied, in a hard, indifferent voice.

She hadn't seen Susan Wall for weeks now. They had argued over the strike, and Mrs Wall had slammed Angie's front door so that the house trembled. Then, the next day, Melanie had knocked on the door, her cheeks scarlet and her eyes sliding about all over the place, so they wouldn't have to rest on Angie's face. She had spoken in a low voice, 'Auntie Angie, I'm sorry . . . Dad says I'm . . . he says I can't come here to babysit, not any more . . . I'm really sorry . . .'

Angie Golding looked at her, then at the empty flower beds. It was very early on in the strike that she had gone down in the morning to bring in the milk, and seen all their carefully-planted flowers pulled up and thrown on the path. That was how it was. People could not hit at the Prime Minister or the leader of the Coal Board, and so they turned their resentment at the people they could see – the police.

There were two sides in Mainthorpe: the police and the working miners and their families, against the strikers and *their* families. She and Melanie were looking at each other now across a massive, invisible barrier that no one could cross. She wanted to shake the girl and tell her to make up her own mind, but knew that would not be fair. It wasn't Melanie's fault. It wasn't anybody's fault.

'How's Rob?' Melanie looked up for the first time, and Angie saw that her eyes were wet.

Impulsively the young woman reached out and gave the girl a hug. 'He's fine, love, but he'll miss you. But don't you worry. All this will be over in a few weeks, my Mick says so. And then we'll all be back to normal.'

'Ohhh, I hope so,' said Melanie miserably.

On both sides of the invisible barrier people realized what was happening to them. But both sides *knew* they were right – and so the differences dug in deeper than ever. Jason Farrell would pass his father in the street without speaking, and only nod curtly at his mother and brother. It was the same in other families. And all the time people would offer each other the small consolation, the solution in which they believed: *that they would be victorious in the end.*

'We'll win, you see,' said Jim Wall over his tea one day. 'The Government won't let this strike go on. They'll make the Coal Board give in. 'Cos the people in the country, they're on our side. They don't want to see our jobs gone, and our communities destroyed.'

'There'll have to be a settlement soon,' said Tony Farrell to Tom. 'The Union will have to give in. Everybody knows we're on a hiding to nothing. People in the South just think we're fools who can't face the truth.'

'It'll all be over soon,' they all agreed.

But of course, it was not so. Easter had come and gone, and April turned into May, and June arrived but still\the strike dragged on. The fresh breezes that always blew around Mainthorpe began to warm, as white and pink and blue flowers blossomed in the hedgerows around the village. The hills looked fresh and misty-green. Despite the skeletal shapes of the pitheads, the ugly fencing and concrete buildings that marked all mines and the dull grey stone of the pit villages, this countryside was beautiful.

Tom Farrell thought so as he roamed the hills one weekend alone. He spotted a kestrel hovering in the clear blue sky, and stood still. It was uncanny the way it could hang there, like a pivot between heaven and earth, defying gravity. He imagined the small furry beast it had seen, a creature whose doom was now sealed, though it might scurry frantically for cover. Then the silent drop, down like a stone, in the split second of an eye's blink. Then death. Tom shivered. The bird was so beautiful, but it was terrible too. That was just one more of the sets of opposites you always had to hold in your mind.

He had grown used to the silence now – a thick absence of sound that surrounded him as surely as it wrapped that waiting bird of prey. Except that he felt more like the small creature on the ground. Nobody spoke to him at school unless they had to. The teachers all knew what was going on, but there was nothing they could do. Tom was tough-minded; he was determined to take it – ever since that day he had been cornered by Lofty Lennard and six or seven others.

'Go on, Farrell, admit it,' said Lofty.

'Admit what?'

'That anybody who goes to work is a lying, snivelling, cowardly, strike-breaking scab who should be shot. Am I right?'

There was a chorus of approval from the other boys. Tom said nothing.

'Am I right, or am I right?' Lofty repeated, standing in front of Tom with his hands on his hips.

'You're not right,' said Tom, 'and you know it.'

Hit him said one voice in his head. But *walk away* said another. Tom clenched his fists inside his pockets, and stood still.

Lofty was laughing. He mimicked Tom's gentle voice. 'Oh, I *know* it, do I? I'll tell you what I know, right enough, Farrell.' His voice changed, and became rough again, as he moved up close to Tom and took hold of his jacket. 'I know you're as big a coward as your dad. I know you're a scab, just like your old man. And I know we don't like scabs round here, do we lads?'

There was a low grumble of agreement from the boys, and they moved in closer, surrounding Tom completely.

'Come on then, Farrell,' said Lofty softly when Tom made no move, 'or are you as chicken as your old man? *He* won't move without the cops to hold his hand.'

Tom was not even aware of his fists coming out of his pockets. He was not in control of his own body – a fury possessed it, turning him into a fighting, flailing, punching, kicking machine. Taken by surprise, Lofty Lennard fell back a pace or two, and Tom was upon him, his right fist landing on Lofty's cheek so that he cried out with pain and anger.

Then he started to fight back. The two boys were well matched so the others did not join in; in any case, there was the code of playground fights at the Ernest Bevin which meant that a group against just one was not allowed.

'You bas-tard, you bas-tard!' panted Tom.

All the anger of the last few weeks, all the frustration

and loneliness, came out in each punch. It wasn't Lofty that Tom was hitting, it was Mainthorpe itself, and the leader of the National Union of Mineworkers, and the Government – *all* of them, everyone and everything.

Lofty grunted, giving ground. A large crowd of kids began to gather round the boys, most of them shouting encouragement to Lofty. Aware of that, even through his red rage, Tom felt lonelier than ever and hit out even harder.

As Lofty stumbled and fell, he felt a surge of triumph, and rushed in, to sit astride the other boy's body. 'You ... take ... back ... what ... you ... said ... about ... my ... dad, all right? *All Right?*' he puffed, holding down Lofty's arms with all his force.

Then something unexpected happened. Lofty let out a cry of anger. 'Yatesy! Mugs! *Get Him!*' And with that his two friends, the tough boys who were always at his side, weighed in, pulling Tom sideways to the floor. It was unfair, everybody knew that, but other boys joined in, and Tom disappeared beneath a pile of tangled limbs.

'Eddy! Lee!' called Tom in his turn.

But nobody came.

He closed his eyes. Blows were landing on his arms and legs, on his back and shoulders. He curled himself into a tight ball, his arms up protecting his head. He felt somebody kick him and winced with pain.

Then there was the sound of running feet, and a voice screamed, 'Get off him! You leave him alone, you, you ...' It was a girl's voice. He felt somebody pushing at the boys who sat on him, rushing round like a small whirlwind, fists flailing, and shouting all the time at the top of her voice, 'Cowards! Cowards! Cowards!'

Curled on the ground, Tom opened one eye – and

saw Melanie Wall in the act of pulling Lofty's longish hair, her face contorted with fury. 'You-get-*off!*' she shrieked.

Suddenly the pushing, scuffling pile fell silent, and Tom opened the other eye. He saw a pair of shiny brown brogues, topped by thick, baggy brown tweed trousers, and his eyes travelled up the body until they encountered Mr Skinner's cold stare.

'What on earth is going on here?' he said, in a tight, hard voice, all the more menacing for being quiet.

Tom scrambled to his feet. His jacket and trousers were torn, and his nose was bleeding. One eye was already starting to close. Lofty was in a similar condition, and stood panting on one side, glaring at Tom as if daring him to tell.

'Farrell!' shouted Mr Skinner. 'Who is responsible for this disgraceful behaviour?'

Tom said nothing. He was still fighting to regain his breath.

'Lennard? *Lennard!*' There was silence.

Melanie stood nearby, her face flushed. In her hand she held a scrap of dark fabric, as if she had clutched somebody's jacket and torn it, pulling the boys off Tom.

Mr Skinner turned to her, frowning. 'I'm sorry to see a girl involved in this sorry fracas, Melanie. But I imagine, since you are involved, that you can tell me who started it?'

She looked at Tom, then at Lofty, then at the ground. 'Er . . . I'm not sure, sir.'

'So you think I should punish both these boys equally – since they were clearly at the root of the trouble?'

Melanie glanced nervously at Tom, 'No, sir . . . I mean . . .'

'Stupid little cow,' muttered a boy in the crowd.

'That's quite enough of that! So – it would seem, from the expression on your face that I would be right in my original guess that it was our usual trouble-maker, our Mr Lennard here who started this fight. Am I right?'

Melanie looked down and said nothing. Mr Skinner started to get really angry. 'Farrell! Lennard! I'm giving you five seconds to answer or the whole form will be in detention. I want to know *who struck the first blow*?'

Lofty grinned, holding the back of his hand to his cut lip and staring at Tom.

'I did, sir,' said Tom wearily.

He saw the look of disappointment and surprise flicker across his teacher's face, before the cold shutter came down. 'Right. You'll both be in detention tomorrow. Tell your parents why. And you, Farrell, come and see me after school today.'

So just after four, when the classrooms had emptied, Tom stood by the form-master's desk. But Mr Skinner looked at him without the anger he had expected.

'You look a mess, lad,' he said.

'I know, sir,' said Tom.

'Look, don't think I don't know what's going on. I didn't have to see that fight from the beginning to guess what happened. Did you really hit him first?' Tom nodded. Mr Skinner shook his head, and spoke more gently than Tom had ever heard him, but gruffly, as if he were embarrassed. 'Look, lad, don't use your *fists*. You're not like the rest of them. You've got words in your head – you hear me, Farrell? *Words*. They'll get you through, when fists will only make things worse. Now you remember that. And here – tidy up the books in the English cupboard with me, so the others think you're doing an extra detention.'

Tom enjoyed that. He loved the piles of dusty dog-eared books: *To Kill a Mockingbird* was the one they were reading and Tom had already read on to the end.

'By the way, Farrell, did you have a go at that competition?'

'Ay Sir, I did. I nearly forgot to post it, though. Don't suppose it got there in time.'

Mr Skinner held up a book that was falling to pieces. 'There's a prize for the school too – of new books. We could do with some here.'

Old Skinny wasn't so bad after all. Since that day he had been his normal self, but Tom noticed him looking gravely at him once or twice, as the hostility of his fellow pupils settled into the long, cold silence. Sometimes, thought Tom, a good punch-up would be better.

The kestrel had disappeared now, tearing the head of some mouse or vole, no doubt. It was magnificent: wild, free and terrible, doing what it liked, when it wanted – the whole world beneath it, in its grasp. Not like their pigeons. They could fly all right, but they were programmed. They had to do what humans had trained them to do, and the rest of the time they were cooped up in their safe little shed. No choices.

Which was he like? With a sudden flash of contempt he saw most of the people he knew as trained pigeons. They did what was expected of them, mostly. People like Jason – terrified of going against the group. 'But Dad's not afraid to be different, and nor am I,' Tom thought proudly. 'The trouble is, it's so lonely.'

He *was* alone. Every day he seemed to move further into isolation, growing used to it. As he gazed into the emptiness of sky all around him, Tom realized that he could stand it simply because sometimes he actually preferred it. He had always felt different to the boys in his class, for reasons he could not explain. And now he didn't have to pretend any more. They had put him outside their fence, and so he was going to learn to live there. The kestrel was alone in the vast sky, and he was alone on the earth, and both were free . . . But no (he corrected his thought), *he* wasn't free. 'But at least I'm independent. At least nobody's telling me what to think anymore,' he said to himself.

Since the fight, Melanie's position in school had been very strange. While Tom was talking to Mr Skinner (kept in by him as an extra punishment, they all thought) she had been cornered by the school gates.

'So you're on the side of the scabs now, are you?' asked Lofty Lennard aggressively, standing in front of her.

There were quite a few girls around, and they joined the group. Even Jackie looked accusingly at Melanie, and called out, 'Your dad wouldn't like it, Mel.'

All afternoon Melanie had been thinking hard. She knew this would happen. Now she was not afraid, nor was she angry – as she had been before. An absolutely icy calm made her straighten her back, fold her arms, and stare levelly at her accusers.

With a quick glance at Jackie that told her to keep out of it, Melanie shrugged. 'So what, Lennard?' she said. He looked surprised. He had expected her to make excuses, or cry, or something.

'Do you want the same as he got?' somebody called.

She looked around, letting her gaze travel very, very slowly, over the faces that encircled her. Some of them – people in her class – could not stand it, and dropped their eyes. That made her feel even stronger. They knew they were wrong.

That's what she had thought out. She still knew that her dad was in the right, and that unless the men stood together and all went on strike, they would have no chance. You *have* to stand together, her mum said, and Melanie agreed. She didn't care that the working miners were shouted at each day; serve them right. But to take it out on their families . . . no, that wasn't right.

That is what she told her classmates. 'You can do what you like,' she said loudly, 'but it won't make it right. It's not my fault what's happening, and it's not Tom Farrell's fault. And in any case . . .' she glared at Billy Yates and Dave Mugford who stood, as always, next to Lofty, 'I thought there was some rules in scraps! I thought it was one to one! That wasn't two against one, even, that was three or four or five against one! You should be ashamed. You should all be ashamed for letting it happen!'

One or two kids drifted away, followed by some more – as if they felt sorry, and did not want to be seen any more with Lofty.

'I'd jump in and try to save anybody who's being picked on, and outnumbered, too,' said Melanie proudly, throwing her head back. 'And I'll do it again too, so there!'

She saw Jackie and the other girls nudge each other, and look at her admiringly. Lofty Lennard and his mates were surprised, she could tell.

'All right, Wallsie, you can be a little heroine,' he sneered, 'But what about your ole' man? Are you going to tell him you're going around with scabs?'

'If you don't, somebody will,' Yatesy muttered.

'Then I'll know who to thank, won't I?' Melanie retorted.

She had worked this one out, too. Her father was, they said, the most powerful man at the mine. Of course, the national leader visited and stood on the picket line, and all the men admired him. But Jim Wall was the man on the spot, with them. He was the one who worked out tactics. All the parents of all the kids who watched her now looked up to her father and respected him.

'All right then,' Melanie continued, 'you tell my dad! I don't care. But I'll tell you one thing for nothing. My dad's as tough as anybody in Mainthorpe, and if there's one thing he wouldn't stand for it would be anybody picking on *me*. No matter what reason. My dad's as loyal as they come – and if you don't believe me, just go home and ask *your* dads!'

'Oh, come on, Lofty,' mumbled Dave Mugford, pulling at the other boy's arm, 'you're wasting your time with *that*.'

This made Melanie come close to losing her temper for the first time. She stepped towards him, clenching a fist and holding it in front of her. 'Don't you call me "that", Dave Mugford, or I'll give you a taste of *this*. I'm not a thing, I'm a person.'

Melanie was about eight inches shorter than the boy, but he said nothing, turning away in disgust. The girls cheered. Fired by this Melanie drew herself up, and marched forward, deliberately pushing Lofty aside. 'Come on then, Jackie,' she said, 'we're missing the telly.' What was left of the crowd scattered before her, and the two girls walked arm in arm through the school gates.

'Ooh, that was great, Mel!' Jackie breathed.

'No thanks to you,' said Melanie sternly.

Her friend accepted the rebuke. 'What are you going to do now, Mel?' she asked humbly.

'What about?'

'Tom Farrell. I mean, are you going to speak to him, or what?'

'That,' said Melanie, 'is *my* business, and I don't want anybody sticking their nose in, not even you, Jackie. All right?'

'All right, Mel,' Jackie had said. And that was that.

CHAPTER SEVEN

Tom Farrell had been sent to Coventry. Melanie had a strong sense of justice, and even though she still agreed with her family on the strike, she knew this was unfair. But Tom wasn't the only one; there were kids in other classes who had the same treatment. But he was the one she knew. He was her friend.

Or was he? She hardly ever spoke to him now, because he avoided everyone. And although Melanie chose sometimes to feel hurt at this, in her heart she was relieved. It didn't put her to the test. That realization made her uneasy.

Her sense of unease would have been made far worse if she had heard the conversation that took place in the Farrells' house one Monday evening, after school. Tom pushed open the kitchen door to find the breakfast dishes still on the table, and his mother sitting staring vacantly into space. He stared disbelievingly at the mess. Something must be badly wrong.

'They spat on her,' she said in a dull voice, not looking at him.

'Who?' he cried. 'Who spat on *who*, Mum?'

'I've been sitting here all day, just thinking about it,' she said. 'I put her to bed, Tom – she was that upset.'

Tom felt that he couldn't bear it. He wanted to scream at her, but kept his voice calm. '*Mum*, tell me properly. What's happened?'

Mrs Farrell turned to him, her eyes puffy and her mouth set in an unusually grim line. 'It was our Linda,' she said in the same flat voice. 'They spat on Linda – and her only a little girl who doesn't really know what it's all about. They were waiting by the school gates, these women – a line of them. And when I walked up with Linda they were shouting at us. '*Scab!*' they were screaming, and *spitting* at us. It was horrible, Tom. Linda . . . she started to cry. So I brought her home. It's all too much for her – Jason leaving, and us all being so down all the time, and, and . . . she couldn't stop crying, love.'

Tom was silent, conscious only of a rage so terrible that he thought his body would burst. What had the strike got to do with Linda? How could she be expected to understand why the world which she thought of as a safe, familiar place, had suddenly turned against her? And how could women – how could *mothers* – be so cruel? He wanted to go out and kick down all the walls of Mainthorpe. Instead he began mechanically to clear the table, and wash up, while his mother sat there, staring at the floor. Then, when it was all done, he wiped his hands and went upstairs to see his sister. To his surprise she was asleep, clutching her doll, its plastic face still streaked with her tears.

Not long afterwards he heard his father's key in the door, and went downstairs to hear his mother repeat her story. Mr Farrell's face, white with strain as it usually was, went dark with anger. 'Who were they?' he demanded. 'I want to know their names.'

'What's the point?' asked Tom's mother wearily.

'I'll go round to their houses! I'll pay them back!' he shouted.

'And I'll come with you, Dad,' added Tom.

'You won't do anything, either of you,' said Mrs Farrell, standing and facing them. 'It'll just make things worse than they already are. Listen to me, Tony! Shall I tell you what you can do, if you want to help? Shall I tell you? Just one thing you can do?' Her voice had risen to near-hysteria.

Mr Farrell heard it, and he spoke quietly. 'What's that, love?'

'You can stay in this house with all the curtains drawn, and not leave it again till all this is over. D'you understand me? Can you get that into your thick, stubborn skull?'

'So you want me to go on strike, is that it?'

'No, not *that*,' she wailed. 'You don't have to go that far. Just go on the sick, or something like that. Just *stay indoors*.'

'If I do that I'll be hiding,' he said quietly, 'and I'll be saying I'm ashamed – that I was wrong all along.'

'Well, what's wrong with that? You're putting your stupid pride above your family, Tony Farrell!'

'Mum!' protested Tom.

'It's all right, son,' said his dad. 'Your mother doesn't mean it. She's had an upsetting day . . .'

'*Upsetting!*' she blazed. 'Is that all you can call it, to walk along the road, and have people all ignoring you, and then hear them calling you all sorts of names? *Upsetting* is it – to have your own little girl spat on outside her school, and her a baby who's done no harm to anyone? If that's all you can call it, Tony, you need to see a doctor as much as I do!'

She sat down heavily. Tom's father sat down too, and Tom saw that he looked a bit ashamed, as well as sad. 'I'm sorry love, I didn't mean . . .'

'No,' she said in a different voice now – a low, sad, tired voice. 'You didn't mean any harm, and I don't suppose those women really knew the harm they were causing. They were just doing what they believe, just like you spend all your time doing what you believe. And so the whole damn miserable thing goes on, with me and Linda caught in the middle.'

'What about the boy?' said her husband, nodding towards Tom.

'Oh, he's a grown lad,' said Mrs Farrell. 'He can look after himself, can't you, love?'

Tom felt the isolation again, as if he was looking at his parents across a gulf. 'No choice, is there?' he replied.

His father looked at him for what seemed like a long time. Then he asked, 'Do *you* think I should stay home, Tom?'

Tom felt his mother's eyes on him, asking him to agree with her. It wasn't *fair*, he thought. Why did he always have to be in the middle, forced to take sides even in his own family? If that was what it meant to be 'grown', then he would rather be Linda. He wanted to shout at them to leave him alone. But he said, 'No, Dad, I don't.'

Mr Farrell looked grateful as he turned to his wife. 'You see, Elaine, you've got to try to understand me – like the lad does. I can't do what you want. I *can't*. All these months they've been calling us cowards, scabs, and worse. I know it's bad for you. This morning . . . (he shook his head and hestitated) . . . Oh, I'd *kill* anyone who touched our Linda. Anyway, I *know* how bad it's been for you, but what about me? You don't know what it's like – going through the picket lines day after day. And listen, you talk of our Linda being innocent, and so she is – but there's women on the pickets bring their two year olds along, and the babies are shouting "Scab!" at us. Two year olds! They don't know what the word means.'

'Shouldn't be there – it's wrong,' Tom muttered.

'There's a lot of things that's wrong, Tom. It's wrong the way the rest of the country doesn't care a

75

damn what's happening up here. They've got their jobs and their houses, and so what do they care about miners being thrown out of work?'

Tom was surprised. 'But I thought . . .' he began.

'Oh ay – I think *this strike*'s wrong – now. But I don't think the reasons for it are wrong, lad. They'll close our pit, and lads in your class'll be on the dole when they leave school, and *that's* not bloody fair. But there's nothing this strike'll do to stop it. Nothing! It's too late. All it's doing is making people hate each other. But I'll tell you this for nothing – we've come this far and we're not turning back!'

'Who's *we*?' asked Tom's mother.

'All of us,' he said. 'We've got to stick together. It'll all be over soon, I'm sure of that. Come autumn and winter the men'll have to go back. It'll get cold, Christmas'll be coming . . . They can't go on. But I'll never be able to look at myself in the mirror again if I don't do what I know is right. I'm walking out that door tomorrow, Elaine, and I want you to be on my side.'

He looked at her. She did not speak.

'Mum?'

Still she said nothing. Then Tom had an idea.

'Tell you what, Mum – I'll make a deal with you. You stick with Dad, and I'll do a job for you – I'll take our Linda to school every day, and I'll do shopping for you as well, so you don't have to go out if you don't want to. They won't give *me* any trouble. And you can sit here with your feet up, OK?'

Then Mrs Farrell smiled a reluctant, pale smile, and said 'Yes'.

That was an important stage for the Farrell family, bringing them closer together. And not long afterwards, something happened to the Walls which had the same effect. It was all about closing ranks against the enemy; knowing for sure which side you were on.

One Saturday, Melanie came back from a morning with Jackie and let herself into the house. She could hear the sound of the vacuum cleaner, almost drowned by loud, heavy metal music. Pushing open the living room door she saw Darren dancing around the room, pushing the Hoover. Melanie grinned, watched for a while, then suddenly switched off his cassette-recorder. He froze, looking up.

'How long have you been there?' he demanded.

'We'll get you a job in the clubs,' she laughed. 'Women'll come from miles around to see the sexy dancing miner who does funny things with the Hoover – oooooh!' And she rolled her eyes cheekily – ducking to avoid the cushion that came hurtling across the room.

'Where's Dad?'

'Gone over to Coulton Main. It's the Michael Garrett demo today. There'll be trouble, I reckon. I'd like to be there myself instead of doing *this*.' And he gave the Hoover a kick.

Melanie was sorry she had switched off his music. He looked happy when she came in, but now his face was bad-tempered. 'Look, Darren, I'll help you and we'll get it all done in no time. I'll put your tape back on,' she said.

They were both watching a film on television much later, when their mother came through the door. Her face was flushed and her eyes sparkled.

'Good meeting?' asked Darren.

'Fantastic. We've made lots of plans, and this woman from London, she was great! There were two others with her, and we all split up into smaller groups and had discussions . . .'

'Good,' said Darren coolly, turning back to the screen.

Melanie made a face at her mum. 'He's in a bit of a bad mood,' she whispered, ''cos Dad decided to go over to Coulton Main and left Darren to get on with the work.'

'Do him good,' smiled Mrs Wall. 'Look what I've got, Mel. This'll cheer him up!'

She put down the bag she was carrying, pulling the paper apart to reveal cream cakes, squashing deliciously together. 'I know it's not Christmas,' she said cheerfully, 'but these women from London – they'd had a collection down there, in their women's groups. So they gave us this money which we all shared out. It was to help us through, like.'

'Dad doesn't like charity payments,' said Darren crossly.

'It's not charity, it's ... it's ... women *giving* to each other,' his mother protested. 'Don't be so mean-minded, Darren!'

'If our Darren's bothered by it, he doesn't have to have a cake,' Melanie said mischievously.

'There's three eclairs so we can all have one. And I'm going to put the kettle on,' said Mrs Wall, walking through into the kitchen.

'Hey, listen!' said Darren, as Melanie rustled the paper bag of cakes. The news had just begun, and he stared intently at the screen.

'There were serious disturbances today at Coulton Main Colliery ... Police and miners clashed in some of the worst scenes of violence ever witnessed during the coal strike ...'

'Mum!' shouted Melanie. Her mother came back, all smiles gone, a worried look on her face.

'The National Union of Mineworkers had arranged a mass rally at the scene of the strike's first casualty. Striking miner Michael Garrett collapsed last week whilst on picket duty at Coulton Main, and died later in hospital. Coronary failure was given as the cause of death. But miners' leaders accuse the police of striking Mr Garrett two hours before he was taken ill ...'

The television screen showed images of men shouting

and waving placards, which said things like **'Murder in a Police State'**, and **'No Police Brutality'**. Then the image shook, as if someone had pushed the cameraman. A policeman's helmet fell off; a miner fell to the ground; faces looked ugly and angry on both sides of the line.

'*Here we go, here we go, here we go,*' sang the demonstrators, as they struggled with the police.

'*Here we go, here we go, here we go,*' sang Darren softly, as he watched.

'Oh, it looks right bad there. I hope our dad's all right,' said Melanie.

Then the telephone rang, making them all jump. Susan picked it up, her eyes fixed on the screen.

'Hello . . . who? . . . oh yes . . . *what?* . . . this afternoon? . . . oh . . . yes, yes . . . I see . . . All right then, thanks for letting me know . . .'

Her face was pale and tense. 'What is it, Mum?' asked Melanie worriedly. 'What's happened?'

Mrs Wall stood facing them, biting her lip, looking as if she hardly heard what her daughter said. Then she folded her arms, hugging them around herself, and looked at them seriously. 'It's Dad – he's been arrested.'

CHAPTER EIGHT

'You should have seen them,' he shouted, almost sobbing with rage. 'Like animals they were. The lads didn't have a chance!'

Mr Wall stood by the fireplace, telling them about the demonstration, and yet his eyes were far away.

'About six of them had one of our lads on the ground and they were punching and kicking him, and I couldn't help myself. I was pulling them off, and next thing – I'm in the police van. Look at that!' He pulled up both sleeves to show huge, mottled bruises. 'They had a go at us with the truncheons, until the Inspector came along.'

Melanie's father had spent a night in the cells, and was then charged with 'obstructing the police'. The Union paid for its men to be bailed, of course, so now Jim Wall was home again. Melanie was glad he was not in prison, but secretly disappointed too. She had imagined him behind bars, and them taking him parcels of food, and him being a sort of hero to the kids in school . . .

'It was unbelievable,' he muttered to Susan, shaking his head. 'The way those coppers charged us you'd have thought we were Germans and it was the war.'

Next day, the Prime Minister made a speech and

referred to the miners on strike as 'the enemy that is within our nation'. When they heard this Mr and Mrs Wall looked at each other in disbelief. *'Enemy?'* shouted Jim Wall. 'This is my country, and I love it as much as anybody does.'

Susan Wall was more quiet. She shook her head, an expression of deep hurt on her face. 'They just don't *know*,' she said, almost to herself. 'They don't understand that we're not asking for anything, we're not wanting *more* – we just want to keep what we've got. Same as anybody.'

Melanie listened, feeling angry. How dare they say things like that about them, when the miners had a right to do what they did? When her dad had been arrested for trying to help somebody else? It must be because the strike had gone on so long, and the country was tired of it. And the reason it had gone on was that men like Tom Farrell's father had stayed working, so that the Coal Board was able to point to them and say the strike wasn't solid. It was all their fault.

The next day, in school, Melanie avoided Tom's eyes altogether.

Every Sunday Melanie and her parents, and sometimes Darren too, would visit old Mrs Wall, who had been moved from the hospital at Doncaster to a much smaller one at Mexton. Most of the people in it were old, and usually Melanie did not want to go. It was not that she didn't love her gran. It was just that she found the place a bit sad.

'It's the old people,' she said to her mother. 'It's like . . . well, they look as though they're just lying there waiting. Nothing else for them to do, except . . .'

She stopped. It was a horrible thing to say, even though it was true. Most true things seemed horrible nowadays.

They sat by the old lady's bed, and talked about the

Prime Minister's accusations. Darren was not with them; he had gone to see the Douglas boys, and Jason Farrell. Melanie could tell that Gran was disappointed not to see her grandson, and that made her sadder than ever.

'They're making out we're all criminals, Gran,' said Susan Wall.

The old lady nodded, her wrinkled hands clutching the sheet in agitation. 'It's always been that way, pet,' she said in her small quavery voice. 'They never understand.'

'Why, Gran?' Melanie asked.

'Tell her, Mother,' said Jim Wall, leaning back uncomfortably in the hospital chair. 'These young ones think it's bad enough now, but it was worse in the old days, wasn't it?'

'Ay, love,' she said, a faraway look in her eye. 'The mines were owned by private men then, Melanie, not by the Coal Board. Rich men. They treated the pitmen worse than animals. And so, if a man tried to lead a strike, he'd be out on the street and his family too. I remember when I was a girl, all our furniture being thrown out in the street by a gang of bullies from Doncaster.'

'But what if it rained?' Melanie gasped.

A faint smile twisted the corners of the old lady's mouth. 'It did, lass. It rained and rained. Neighbours took us in and that – but it weren't just *us*, it were whole streets of us. And then there were the pit accidents. Owners, they didn't bother about safety, even when they were told to sink extra shafts, and that. So there'd be a sort of rumble underground, and it'd be like ... like the earth had stopped turning for a few minutes. Then we'd all run to the pit head, all the women and children, and just wait and wait. No crying, mind. Just waiting.'

Melanie was silent. She had heard most of this

before, but Gran's stories always transfixed her, just as they did her parents – who sat now, staring at the old woman's face, at the eyes which gazed deep into the past.

'That's what it were like that day, and my mother knew – I could tell she knew. She stood with her shawl over her head, praying. I can still hear the words: *Dear Lord, please let Jimmy be safe, please let Jimmy be safe* . . . Over and over. Hours we stood there. And me holding her hand while I don't think she knew I was there. Mmmmm.' She shook her head slowly from side to side, and moisture filmed her eyes.

'Scabs should hear all this,' muttered Jim. 'Then they'd remember what they owe the Union. Then they'd be shamed before they'd cross a picket line.'

But his mother carried on as if no one had spoken. 'They didn't bring the men out for two days. Then we laid my father out in the front parlour, and she washed him clean, and dressed him in his best suit for burial. She made him look lovely – all clean and new as if he'd never been underground. And she said to me afterwards, "Jeannie, you promise me you'll never marry a miner." And I said to her, "Mum, I *want* to marry somebody like our dad." And I did – didn't I, Jim?'

She reached for her son's hand, and Jim Wall looked at her smiling. 'Ay, mother, my dad was a great man.'

'He was just like my father, and you're just like him, lad. All fighters – all of you. And good luck to you, I say. Only . . .'

'What, Mother?'

'Only . . . don't wear yourself out fighting things that you can't do anything about.'

'But you can! You have to try!' Jim Wall protested.

The old woman sighed. 'Oh, I know what you mean, son, and I'm behind you. It's just that I think of my father, buried alive down there, and then your father who coughed his life out before his time, and now there's you and our Darren, and ... I don't know. I wonder sometimes if it's worth it.'

Melanie's father shrugged. 'There's nothing else, is there, Mother?'

'Do you think I'll marry a miner, Mum? Like Gran and you?' asked Melanie.

Both women looked at her, and smiled. 'Have you got anybody in mind, lovey?' asked Gran.

Melanie blushed. 'No, 'course not!'

'Well, I don't think you will,' said Mrs Wall decisively. 'I think you'll study hard at school and get your exams, and get a good job away from here.'

Jim Wall reached across and ruffled his daughter's hair. 'Oh, I don't think old Curly here will go very far from home,' he said fondly, 'and I don't want her to, either.'

'There's nothing wrong with marrying a miner,' said Gran with the distant look back in her eyes. 'I'd take my Jimmy all over again, even though times were hard.'

Susan Wall frowned slightly. 'Well, I think we should look further,' she said sharply. 'And all this talk about marrying miners is all very well, *if* there's any jobs left for the men by the time she's twenty.'

''Course there will, woman,' said her husband, with an equal sharpness. 'Because that's what we're fighting for. And we're going to win, you see.'

Gran Wall looked from one to the other. She saw Melanie glance miserably down at the bedclothes. 'Will you do something for me, pet?' she said softly, 'Will you pass me my bag that's in the locker there?'

Melanie did as she was asked. Gran fished inside the old bulging handbag in which she kept all her 'papers'. Its clasp was held together with an elastic band.

'Here, Susan,' she said, holding out an envelope to her daughter-in-law.

'What is it?'

'It's my savings, pet, that's what it is. I've taken everything out, and I want you to have it. To see you through this patch. I know things must be getting hard at home, with the housekeeping. I won't see my family short.'

'Oh, no, Mother, I'm not taking your money,' Jim Wall protested, standing up. His face was crimson with embarrassment.

'Why not!' said the old woman, in a voice that was suddenly strong and more determined than her son's. 'It's mine to give as and when I want to, Jim, and you remember that. You're on strike, and I'm stuck in here, and you need money and I don't. So that's all there is to it. There's three hundred pounds in there, and it won't go very far with today's prices – but it'll mean you can get some decent Sunday roasts for the children, and put some aside for Christmas. And don't you argue, lad!'

Susan Wall leaned across the bed and kissed her mother-in-law shyly on the cheek. Then she tucked the envelope in her own handbag. 'Thanks, Gran,' she whispered in a husky voice. 'That's a lovely help, it really is. It'll make all the difference at home.'

CHAPTER NINE

The summer was grey and muggy mostly, and people longed for the clouds to lift. The air was heavy. Showers of rain would fall, giving some relief, and occasionally summer lightning lit the gaunt pit-head gear with a flash of yellow.

The strike, too, settled on Mainthorpe, like a permanent cloud. The men and women who believed passionately in the rightness of their cause still longed for an ending. They wanted to *win*, though, and couldn't accept any other possibility – despite the price that was paid on both sides. Some people moved away from Mainthorpe for good. And sometimes Melanie felt that they were the lucky ones. The news was worse and worse every day; the violence increased as tempers were shortened by heat and boredom.

As August dragged on, Susan Wall came home telling stories of hardship amongst families, especially those with small children. 'But it'll be worse in the winter, mind,' she would say – making arrangements with her Women's Group to take food parcels to those who needed them most. Nobody ate very well; the children would long for pork or lamb chops, but eat potatoes, and perhaps a slice of bacon – just as (although they did not know it) their grandparents and great-grandparents had done.

Nobody went on holiday, except to stay with relatives when they could. Melanie's fourteenth birthday came and went. Thanks to Gran she got a new pair of blue jeans, and (best of all) a matching jacket. Darren gave her a pair of earrings, in the shape of tiny dark blue hearts. When she protested he reassured her that they were cheap, from Mexton market. 'I wouldn't spend much on you, Mel!' he joked – and seemed, for a few seconds, like the happy-go-lucky big brother who liked to give her extra money. For Darren had changed. He'd reverted to the way he used to be a long time ago, when he was bunking off from school all the time, and wanting to fight everybody. Dark, somehow, inside himself – that's how Melanie remembered him then. Now he was like that again. He was sullen, and had even started to quarrel with his father about 'tactics'.

'You're a hothead, Darren, and no good'll come of it,' warned Mr Wall.

Feeling uneasy, Melanie felt that something was brewing. And so for once she longed for school to start – anything to break the dreadful monotony of the days.

On the first day of the autumn term Tom Farrell was summoned to the Headmaster's study. He knew he had done nothing wrong, and was not surprised to see Mr Skinner sitting there too, with Mrs Bennett, Tom's new form teacher.

Tom stood in front of the desk, while Mr Entwhistle beamed at him, arms folded.

'We're very proud of you, Farrell ... He's a credit to your teaching, Mr Skinner.'

'He's done well, Headmaster,' said Mr Skinner simply.

Tom stared at them, with no idea what they were talking about. Mr Entwhistle stood up, reached across the desk, and held out his hand. 'You've obviously

forgotten all about it, laddie! Well, we've had a letter
this morning with the best news we've heard this year.
You've won first prize in your age group, Farrell! Well
done!'

He held out a letter for Tom to read, but though
Tom took it the words made no sense. Mr Skinner was
talking . . . explaining. He knew he had been right to
make Tom enter the writing competition, and now
Tom was to go to London to a grand prize giving, and
collect the prize money for himself and for the school.

'On my own, sir?' asked Tom, suddenly nervous.

'No, you can take one of your parents, and all the
fares will be paid. It'll be a grand day out,' said Mr
Entwhistle. He glanced down at the letter, and
chuckled. Tom had never seen the Head (usually a
cool, distant man) look so jolly. 'Two hundred
pounds-worth of books for the school, and fifty pounds
for you, lad. Have you thought what you'll spend it
on?'

'No, sir.'

'Take my advice and put it in the post office.
There'll be plenty of rainy days. Now we must make
an announcement in Assembly.'

'*No!* . . . er, sir.'

The Head looked surprised, and so did the two
teachers. 'Why not?' asked Mrs Bennett.

'I'd . . . I just don't want people to know,' said
Tom.

'Nonsense, lad! You're a credit to the school. It's
the first time anyone from Ernest Bevin has ever won
something. It puts us on a national stage!' Mr Entwhistle got up decisively.

But Mr Skinner was looking at Tom with a little
more understanding. 'You don't want to stand out, is
that it, Tom?'

Tom nodded, looking gratefully at his English
teacher.

'Can I have a word with you, Headmaster?' said Mr Skinner, nodding at Tom that he was dismissed.

So the Headmaster announced that Tom Farrell had won the first prize in his age group in the National Essay Competition, gaining two hundred pounds for the school. He made no mention of Tom's own prize, nor did he say that the prize money was to come in the form of books – because Mr Skinner, coldly realistic as he was, thought there might be less excitement.

To Tom's amazement there was a small ragged cheer – just as there might have been months ago, before the strike. And as they walked to lessons, pupils came up and congratulated him – girls, mainly, but it still made him feel good inside. As if he was starting to be forgiven . . .

Most of the kids in the school were genuinely pleased. At last something good had happened, and to one of *them*. Because Tom had won something for the school he had won it for everyone, and so – in a funny way – they felt like prizewinners themselves. Of course Lofty and all the other lads who had sent him to Coventry said jeering things about 'Goody-goody swots' in his hearing, but it made no difference to him. Tom realized that no words anyone could say had the power to hurt him anymore.

'Always said he had brains,' said Eddy.

'Be writing a book next!' said Lee.

'Yeah, make sure there's lots of sex and violence in it,' said Eddy, digging Tom in the ribs. 'That way you'll get rich.'

'Well done, Tom,' said Melanie shyly, coming up behind them.

He felt absurdly pleased and awkward. 'Thanks,' he said, shifting his old bag on his shoulder. Eddy nudged Lee slyly, grinning broadly at Melanie. 'You never told us what you wrote about, Farrell,' he said. 'Was it a love story?'

'No,' said Tom, steering her ahead of them along the corridor. 'If you must know, it was about the strike. What else?'

The best part of it all was telling his parents. Tom's mother looked as if she would burst with pride, and his father echoed Mr Entwhistle's words: 'Best thing that's happened this year.'

'That isn't very hard, though, is it?' said Tom.

The Saturday of the prize giving arrived. Mr Farrell wore his best suit, and managed to persuade Tom to wear a tie. There were tears of happiness in his mother's eyes as she kissed them goodbye. Since the news that he had won, she had been stronger and far more cheerful. 'You've given me a tonic, love,' she said.

On the train they talked about the pigeons, and looked out of the window, and read newspapers, and ate the sandwiches Mrs Farrell had prepared. Tony Farrell had been to London once before, but it was all new to Tom, and he gazed about at the red buses, the black taxis, and the extraordinary choked tangle of cars, vans, motorbikes, and small lorries.

'That's never traffic – it doesn't *move*,' he said to his father, as they studied the map outside the Tube station.

It was like a dream, unfolding very slowly, in which Tom was playing a starring role, but knowing all the while (as you rarely do in dreams) that he would wake up soon and it would all be over. It was the isolation again. Oh yes, he was pleased to have won, but not as pleased as his family and teachers were. It was as if he had passed beyond everything, into a world of his own.

The prize giving was at a large hotel in central London, and after lunch the ceremony began. A man stood up: '. . . And now I would like to call upon our Chairman, Lord Grafton, to present this year's awards . . .' Everybody applauded enthusiastically.

The winners in each of the age ranges (there was one above and one below Tom's) sat with their parents on one large table; the runners-up at two other tables. There were journalists and childrens' book publishers, and people who worked for the chain of bookshops whose competition it was . . . and Tom felt bewildered. All the noise and congratulations, and the crisp white tablecloths, and the wonderful smell of roast lamb and potatoes – and all this because he had sat down and written what he felt about what was going on around him. That was all. Simple, really – and not worth all this fuss.

'We chose Tom Farrell's essay from a record entry in the thirteen to sixteen age group, because of its unusual combination of passion and clarity. From the heart of a troubled part of England, from the very front line of this terrible miners' strike, came this moving plea for *fairness*, and for the right of men to make choices . . .'

Tom felt his father looking at him proudly, and bent his head to examine his nails. But he had to rise, and go up to the platform – his face scarlet. People were clapping, then there were more speeches. But the voices merged into an indistinct murmur around him, as – with sudden clarity– he thought longingly of home. At last the formalities were over, and people milled around.

'And what do you want to be when you leave school?'

The man who had presented the prizes, Lord Grafton, was large, with a pink face against which his shock of white hair made a pleasing contrast. A pale blue silk handkerchief peeped from the breast pocket of his grey pinstriped suit. He looked wealthy – there was a kind of gloss to his face and his clothes, and a confidence to his manner that Tom recognized. He had seen it on the television. It belonged to men and women who were successful, who *ran* things. His dad didn't have it. Nobody in Mainthorpe had it.

'Dunno, really,' he mumbled.

'Tom! Answer properly, lad!' said his father.

'I suppose it's hard for them to know, Mr Farrell. But this boy shows a real talent for writing. Maybe he'd like to join a newspaper, or something like that?'

'Ay, maybe,' said Tony Farrell, while Tom stood dumbly by his side. 'We'll see. But it seems right strange to be talking about choosing. Where we're from the kids do one thing or the other, and there's not much else. Worries me what the lad'll do. Me and the wife, we want him to go to college and get qualifications, and we think he will. Hope so, anyway. But sometimes the other kids put ideas in their heads and they want to leave school and start work. You know what it's like.'

Tom thought that this rich bloke could not possibly know what it was like, but he was nodding sympathetically, and looking at Tom with kind eyes.

'And what have you got to say about all this?'

Tom shrugged. 'There's not many jobs in the north,' he said shortly. 'Just ask my dad.'

'Yes . . . er . . . I seem to remember gathering, from reading your son's essay, that you are one of the working miners, Mr Farrell, is that correct?'

'Ay, that's right,' said Tony, standing straight.

'I do admire you most wholeheartedly,' said the man, putting out his hand. Tony Farrell shook it firmly. 'Thank you very much.'

'And do you think the Coal Board ought to negotiate again?'

Tom was surprised and pleased to hear Lord Grafton asking *his* dad a question – as if he really wanted to know his opinion.

'Ay, I reckon they should, you see the problem is . . .'

Tom wandered off, leaving them talking about the progress of the strike. He felt confused. He was glad his dad had met someone who seemed to understand, and yet it annoyed him, too. What did that man know about Mainthorpe, and what it would be like there if the mine closed? He had not the faintest idea – because Mainthorpe seemed on another planet when you were down here. Nobody here, in this lovely room with pink plush curtains, and glittering china and glass, could possibly know.

He was glancing down at the leather-bound book of short stories they had given him, with his cheque tucked inside, when he felt someone tap his arm. A girl was standing next to him, a girl who was almost as tall as he was, with long fair hair tied in a ragged pony-tail on top of her head, so that it cascaded down to one side. He knew that the untidiness was deliberate; the girl was dressed in fashionable black clothes and wore make-up and dangling silver earrings. He guessed she was about his age, although she looked older.

'Well done!' she said. 'I've been wanting to talk to you.'

'Well ... uh ... *you* did pretty well to get third prize,' said Tom, feeling self-conscious.

The girl's voice made him feel terrible; it rang out clear and confident, with long pure vowels, and a kind of musical swooping sound. It was the kind of voice that assumed people would want to hear it, and because of that it would go through life *being* heard. It made Tom feel grubby and mumbling, somehow.

'Oh that,' said the girl, waving a dismissive hand at her own achievement. 'Not particularly good; English's my best subject. Is it yours?' Tom nodded. 'By the way, my name's Rose, but people call me Rosie. You're Tom, I remember when they called it out. What school do you go to?'

'Ernest Bevin Comprehensive. That's in Mainthorpe.'

'Yorkshire?'

Tom nodded.

'How lovely.'

'Not when you're there. What's your school called?'

'St Catherine's Ladies' College.'

'Oh.'

'I've been meaning to ask you – is it really terrible where you live? All that fighting we see on the news? And the police being attacked, and everything?'

'Things happen you don't see on the news,' said Tom shortly.

'Oh? What sort of things?'

'Well, just put it this way – the police do bad things, too. There's people been beaten up by the police, and women sworn at, just for standing on a picket line . . .'

'Well, they shouldn't be there really, should they?' Rosie's tone was confident: she expected him to agree with her.

'Why shouldn't they be there?' he asked, irritated. She looked at him in amazement.

'But I thought . . .?' She looked across the room to where Tony Farrell was still deep in conversation with Lord Grafton.

Tom realized that it had been quite clear from the little speech about his essay that his family was against the strike. In fact, he remembered a sort of ripple of approval that ran through that splendid room. He had felt proud, then. But for reasons he did not understand, he felt uncomfortable now.

'Look, Rosie,' he said, 'whatever you thought, you thought wrong, OK? My family's had a bad time in this strike, but that doesn't mean I hate the rest of them. Those women – like my friend Melanie's mum – they're doing something they believe in. You don't know what it's like when there's no jobs in a place . . .'

'But can't people move, and get jobs?' she interrupted, her eyes wide.

'What with? Where do they live when they move? It takes money to move house, and in any case – it's not easy for a man to find other work when he's been a miner all his life. Anyway, people get set in a place . . . Oh – forget it!'

'Well, there's no need to be rude.'

'I'm sorry.'

She shrugged and moved away. Tom stood alone, feeling lumpy and coarse, clutching his book and listening to the warm, satisfied sound of the conversation around him as it rose to the ornate ceiling and glittering chandelier. Nobody would understand, even if he spent hours trying to explain. 'Kids in school were right – it *is* another world down here,' he thought, longing to be on the train pulling out of Kings Cross Station.

He wandered back to his father, whose face was alight. 'It's a grand car. Best they ever made,' he was saying.

'You would love the Bentley. She still handles like a dream,' said Lord Grafton. 'Anyway, you think this might be a possibility? You know I would like to do something to help.'

Lord Grafton was looking at Tony Farrell with a keen and questioning expression. But Tom's father saw that Tom was listening, and raised a hand to the Chairman, as if telling him not to say any more. 'All right,' said Lord Grafton. 'Shall I telephone you in a week or two?'

'Sorry, we're not on the phone,' said Mr Farrell.

'Ah . . . well, not to worry, here's my card. You will get in touch, won't you?'

He held out a small oblong of cardboard, which Tony Farrell took, turning it over in his hand. Tom stared at it too, impressed. He could not imagine why his father had become so friendly with the most important man in the room.

And his father looked different somehow – stronger, more relaxed. He was the first to hold out his rough, red hand and grasp the softer, whiter hand Lord Grafton offered in response. He nodded with a broad smile. 'I'll do that. You can be sure of that, sir.'

The train pulled through bleak backs of houses and wastes of track in North London, gathering speed as it passed stark tower blocks and walls daubed with graffiti. Tom took off his tie and bundled it in his pocket, leaning back with relief. 'I'm glad that's over,' he said.

'Why, lad? It was great. I was right proud of you, too. I only wish your mother could have seen it all.'

'She'd have been nervous.'

'Ay, maybe she would.' Tom's father fell silent, looking out of the window with a thoughtful air. At last Tom asked what he was thinking about.

'Oh, not much. Just wondering . . .'

'About what?'

'Just things. I'll tell you . . .'

'You got very friendly with that posh bloke.'

'Ay, and why not? He's got this collection of vintage cars, on his estate. It's a sort of museum. People pay to go and see them.'

Tom grinned. He knew his father's obsessions. 'Oh, no wonder you got on so well.'

'He didn't expect to meet someone there who knows so much about the cars,' said his father.

Then he picked up the evening paper, read for a few minutes, but soon put it down again. And after that Mr Farrell spoke very little. Tom started to read the book of short stories, putting the cheque carefully in his pocket first. From time to time he glanced up at his father, noticing how thin he had become, and how there seemed to be more lines of worry on his face these days. Yet he looked happier than he had for months, and almost, in a strange way, *triumphant*. A quiet smile curled at the corners of Tom's father's mouth as he stared at the passing landscape and townscape, all the way back to Doncaster.

CHAPTER TEN

'What *sort* of job?' asked Tom in disbelief.

His parents sat each side of the fireplace; Linda on their father's knee. They were looking at him with bright, expectant faces. Suddenly he felt again (as happened more and more these days) as if he were the parent and they were the children. Ever since the trip to London two weeks ago, Mr and Mrs Farrell had been behaving as children do when Christmas draws near: full of suppressed excitement and whispers.

Mr Farrell took a deep breath. 'You know I told you about Lord Grafton's collection of cars – the Motor Museum? Well, he wants me to go and look after it. It's a stroke of luck for me, Tom. The man who's been maintaining them is leaving; and after we'd talked he said he was sure I could do the job. It's something I wouldn't have dreamt of!'

'But . . . where would we live?'

Mrs Farrell beamed. 'There's a cottage, Tom, a real country cottage! On the estate. It goes with the job. He says in his letter (she read from the piece of paper she held in her hand), 'My wife says that you will find Sunnybank Cottage very comfortable. There are three bedrooms, and the kitchen was newly fitted last year.' Oh, Tom, it's got *central heating* too!'

'I want to live in a little cottage – like Snow White,' said Linda, taking her thumb from her mouth and smiling at the thought of the adventure.

Tom stared at them. So this was the meaning of the letter that had been seized quickly by his father, as a starving man might clutch at a piece of bread.

'But . . . where *is* all this?' he asked.

'Just outside a town called Iver – in Buckinghamshire. We'll be able to go to London – see all the sights!'

'In all that traffic?' cried Tom. 'You'd never find your way, Dad!'

His father laughed. 'Of course I would! You can get used to anything when you try. When you want to.'

'Do you want to, then?'

''Course I do, and so does your mother!' (She nodded vigorously.) 'We've *had* it up here, Tom. At that prize giving Lord Grafton told me there might be a chance of this job, if I was interested, and – all right – I admit I was suspicious at first. But what a chance! I couldn't believe it. A job, and a house thrown in . . . We thought about it a lot, your mother and me, and talked about it a lot – and we've decided it's the best thing for you and Linda. There's a really good school for you just a mile away – Lord Grafton said – and they've got a proper sixth form and get lots of lads and lasses into college, and university too, each year. It's a chance for you, Tom!'

'But what about me?' Tom asked.

His father looked puzzled: 'It's you I'm talking about!'

'But . . . I mean, you say you've decided, but what about me? What if I don't want to go?'

'Don't be daft, lad!'

'I'm not daft, I mean it. I like it here. We belong here.'

'Oh yes,' said his mother, a note of bitterness creeping into her voice, 'we've got such a lot of friends in Mainthorpe. I can't hardly walk down the street without them coming up and talking to me. Makes me feel all warm inside, to think I belong to this *lovely community . . .*'

'Oh, that's just *now*, Mum. When the strike's over . . .'

'When it's over, do you think they'll *forget?*' she asked harshly. 'Do you think our life here'll ever be like it was before? I'm surprised at you, Tom. I thought you knew better!'

'It's a *chance* – a chance for us all,' said Mr Farrell softly, cuddling Linda close but never taking his eyes off his son.

Tom felt resistance close over him like a shell. Why should he just agree with them? Why should he agree to being uprooted, just because some posh Lord had tried to interfere in their lives?

'I don't care if it's a chance or not. I don't see why we have to move somewhere we don't belong. And you, Dad – you'd miss being a proper miner – a *man's* job – that's what you used to call it.'

His father flushed at that. 'Ay,' he said, 'I used to think it was a man's job. But crawling under the ground in the dark, eating sandwiches covered in dust, sweating, deaf with the noise of the machinery . . . You think that's a proper job, do you? All right lad, do *you* want to do it?' Tom shook his head. 'No – no you don't. And you're right. If Lord Grafton offers me a decent wage for a decent job, and respects me like he says he does, then I'll work decently for him. There's more dignity in that than there is in being a worm under the ground like I am now. Who respects me now? The men don't!'

'The Coal Board – and most of the country!' Tom shouted.

After all, wasn't it believing that – in the *rightness* of it – that had kept them going?

'Rubbish! Don't be pathetic! They don't care two hoots about me or what I do, unless it's a bit useful to them like it is now. When the men have to go back to work you see what'll happen. This pit will close, like they said it would, and do you think someone will tell me I've been a good boy and can have a job? Of course they won't!'

Tom hung his head, shocked to hear his father talk that way. His mother was looking distressed, but she smiled with relief when Linda said brightly, 'Will I be able to have a garden of my own? I want to grow flowers.'

'And vegetables – we'll grow all our own vegetables,' said Mrs Farrell enthusiastically.

Linda made a face. 'Don't want to grow veggy-troubles.'

'You'll be able to grow flowers, love – if your big brother says you can,' said Mr Farrell gently.

'It's not up to the boy, Tony,' said Tom's mother.

'Well, it's for him to say he wants to move. I'm not forcing him. He's stood by me all these months, and it's not right if I uproot him now without him wanting.'

Tom was horrified. He did not want to make the decision. Panic rose in his chest . . . He felt afraid. His father was looking at him, questioningly.

'Tom,' he said in a persuasive voice, 'what is there for *you* to stay for?'

Tom hesitated. Then he gulped, 'My friends.'

'Who do you mean – exactly?' his father asked.

'Oh, kids at school. Lee and Eddie, and . . .'

His father was relentless. 'You know as well as I do that they haven't been round like they used to. I've noticed, Tom! Because I know it's my fault, and it's made me feel terrible.' He sighed. 'No point in going over all that again. Who else is there, Tom?'

Tom was silent. Then, to his embarrassment, Linda piped up, 'Melanie Wall. She's his friend.'

'Don't be daft,' said Tom sharply. 'I hardly speak to her.'

It was true. Since the beginning of term it seemed that Melanie was keeping away from him. He could only imagine that her parents had ordered her to, since she wouldn't be like that herself. Yet ... even the feeling of distant friendliness had disappeared. It hurt his feelings – though not as much as he would have thought. *You have to toughen yourself*, Tom told himself, *and then no one can hurt you*. Coping with the new sense that Melanie had drifted away from him – and that she could not help it – Tom realized that he was growing up. It was rather a bleak feeling.

His father was frowning. 'I'm glad to hear it – and I should keep it that way. If I were you I'd keep well away from her, Tom.'

'Why?'

'Because that family . . .'

Tom's mood changed; he was angry now, and leapt to Melanie's defence. 'What *about* her family?' he burst out, knowing the answer quite well. 'And anyway, what's that got to do with her?'

'If it wasn't for Jim Wall . . . oh, never mind him. I suppose he's doing what he believes in. But that Darren, he's a young thug, and he'll get himself into serious trouble soon, you see. I don't want you hanging round with any of them, you hear me?'

'No,' said Tom, 'I don't hear you.'

He stared at his father in disbelief. It was as if they were all suspended there, for a few seconds, staring down into a big black gulf between them, which threatened to grow wider – swallowing everything up. Tom felt that if he said any more he would be widening that gulf, which threatened the happiness of his family. And family was more important than any friendship, wasn't it?

Just at that moment, the doorbell rang.

CHAPTER ELEVEN

Melanie had arrived home from school that night to find her parents talking about vandalism. The newspapers had been full of stories of walls daubed, gates broken and buildings set fire to at collieries all over the country. 'It's just plain daft,' said Jim Wall, folding up his paper with a decisive movement. 'Like cutting off your nose to spite your face.'

'Yes, love, I know, but the young lads are so frustrated they'd do anything,' explained Mrs Wall.

Darren sat sulkily in the corner, saying nothing.

'Susan – it's bad for us *all*. People all around the country who're sympathetic – they get put off when they read about smashing the machinery and all that. Vandalism's vandalism – and these pits'll have to be worked when all this is over. And as for chucking lumps of concrete at police cars . . . it loses all sympathy.' He shook his head.

'We don't need their stupid sympathy,' growled Darren.

'Of *course* we do!' retorted his father testily. 'People are feeling this strike's gone on too long. They think the Government's handling it badly. If young louts go round causing damage, they'll change their minds – and then we haven't got a hope of winning!'

'Haven't got a hope anyway,' said Darren, rising to his feet and leaving the room without another word.

There was a silence. Mrs Wall looked worried. 'I don't know what's got into our Darren,' she said, 'but he's acting awfully strangely.'

'I hope he keeps himself out of trouble,' said her husband.

Melanie thought it was stupid to smash things. She couldn't understand it when the boys from the youth club went wild sometimes, and tried to bend fences, or smash bollards for no reason at all. 'Like little kids,' she thought – remembering, suddenly, how little Rob Golding, even at two, would smash his toy cars together. She had not seen him for months now. It made her sad.

Her mother sighed. 'Trouble is, reading about it, or hearing it on the news puts ideas in their heads. They're bored enough, and what with no money, and all these police all over the place ... Been nothing done at Mainthorpe, though, has there?'

'No,' said Jim Wall, 'not yet. There's talk of a gang going all over the place, trying to destroy the machinery. There was a lot of damage over at Sefton and at Endbury. If they try to do Mainthorpe, they'll be asking for it. I heard today that more police reinforcements are coming in. They wouldn't have a chance.'

Mrs Wall nodded in agreement. She was carefully transferring piles of leaflets from the box they had arrived in, to a large bag. Melanie picked one up. 'Miners' Wives and Families Appeal', it said.

'Annie's taking these over to Mexton tonight, Jim. I'm meeting her in the Club. Why don't you come and we can have a drink? You'll be all right, won't you Mel?'

''Course. I've got to do my homework. We've got a whole pile.'

About an hour later Melanie was lounging on her

bed, school books all round her, listening to the radio and trying hard to concentrate on her homework at the same time. It was a losing battle.

She heard Darren's key in the lock and was about to go down to greet him when she realized he was with someone.

'Dad! Mum!' he called. Then, when there was no reply, he spoke to his companion: 'Great – they're out.'

She heard him go through to put the kettle on and could not resist her curiosity any longer. When she bounded down the stairs she saw Jason Farrell and Pete Douglas sitting in the living room.

'Hey up!' she called. Melanie could not help enjoying it when her brother brought friends home, although she had to admit that Jason Farrell was not nearly as good-looking as his brother.

Darren brought mugs of tea through, and they chatted idly for a few minutes. Then he told Melanie to go back upstairs and get on with her homework. It was not unfriendly, but something in his face made her suspicious. It was a suppressed excitement, she thought – and Jason and Pete shared it. They all looked on edge, wanting her gone.

Back in her room she did her best to concentrate on the maths, but could not. She switched off the radio, telling herself that would help – but knowing in her heart she wanted a chance to hear what was going on downstairs. It was hard. Nothing but indistinct mumbles, and from time to time a clearer sentence as one of the boys raised his voice. *Why shouldn't we?* she heard.

Melanie opened her door a fraction, then a bit more. She moved stealthily, avoiding the floorboard that always creaked, and settled down with her ear to the crack.

'It's gone on long enough,' Darren was saying. 'I'm fed up with nothing happening.'

'Too right,' murmured the other two, still sounding a bit dubious.

Darren's voice was decisive: 'No, they'll be patrolling there. I've worked it out. We get a couple of the lads from the pub to start something, maybe, just where West Lane joins Mexton Road, and while the cops are sorting that out we cut across the fields to that bit of fencing behind the canteen. We take the wire cutters . . .'

'Easy,' said Jason.

'Work our way through – you know, there's plenty of cover, like – and then we'll see to the winding gear. Take tools strapped round our chests, and it'll be no problem.'

'Smash it up good and proper,' added Jason, with satisfaction.

Melanie gasped. *The winding gear!* The mechanism which carried the cage and its cargo of men up and down, from the surface to the bottom. Melanie was enough of a miner's daughter to know how important it was. And that knowledge added to her horror of what Darren, of all people, was suggesting.

'What about the petrol?' asked Pete.

'I'll bring that,' Darren replied. 'Just enough for a small fire – so they know we mean business.'

Melanie caught her breath. Darren *couldn't*! He would be caught, and be sent to prison. Dad would be furious, and Mum would be upset . . . In any case, it was bad for *all* of them, Dad had said so. Bad for the cause. It made people think the miners were just a lot of destructive louts . . . But what could she do? She knew she could not stop them on her own. If only she could think of a plan.

She listened again. They were deciding that the best time would be well before the pub closed, because the police expected trouble late, not early. She heard Darren go out the back again, to where Dad kept the tool box, and then she jumped. Darren was calling her.

Melanie clattered downstairs. Darren grinned at her, looking so much like his old self that she relaxed for a moment.

'We're just off down the pub for a game of darts,' he said.

'I thought you didn't have any beer money,' she muttered.

'Doesn't cost to play darts, and in any case, old Jack gives us credit,' said her brother, putting on his donkey jacket.

'Why don't you stay in with me, Darren, and play cards? I'm fed up being on my own.'

'Go on, Darren, be a nice kind babysitter,' joked Pete Douglas.

'Some baby! She's fourteen now,' said Darren.

'Yeah ... and have you seen anything of *my* baby brother lately?' asked Jason, in a not-too-pleasant voice.

'Be funny if I didn't, seeing as we're in the same class,' Melanie retorted.

'Does his halo still fit him then?' said Jason. 'I'd have thought it'd got tight lately, what with all these superstar trips to London.'

'*One* trip to London, that's all, and you know it, Jason Farrell.' It was natural, she realized, to jump to Tom's defence.

'Come on, let's go,' said Darren, heading for the door.

When they had gone, Melanie felt small and alone. Panicking, she thought of going to the Club and telling her parents. Immediately, she dismissed the idea. She could not go against the 'training' that was in them all – that whatever happened, you didn't *tell*. Darren would never forgive her for being a sneak – or a 'grass' as they said on the police films on television.

But she had to stop him somehow – even if not for his own sake. For her father's. That was it. How could Jim Wall go on being a responsible leader (as he was always saying to Susan) if his son had done something like that? No, thought Melanie, she wouldn't let him disgrace Dad.

But what on earth should she do? She chewed her nail for a few moments, staring absentmindedly at her pale reflection in the mirror. She raised her hand to her hair, thinking what a mess it looked – straight at the roots but breaking into straggly curls at the ends. Her hand stopped in the middle of the movement, and she smiled. A memory of something that seemed an age ago ... It was then that Melanie knew that she needed help – and that there was only one person to give it. She knew she must go to Tom's house.

Tom opened the door, glad to escape from the living room – and stared at the sight before him. Melanie stood, hands in her anorak pockets, eyes wide – and a look of urgency about her he had never seen before.

'Hey up, Mel! What're *you* doing here?' he whispered, stepping outside and holding the door closed behind him.

'Tom, I've got to talk to you! Something's going to happen!'

He decided in an instant. 'Go to the end of the path. I'll get my jacket,' he hissed – and in a few seconds it was done. He knew, as he closed the door behind him, that his parents would be angry and upset that he had gone off in a huff. But he couldn't help that.

Quickly he marched her along the road, until they were a safe distance from the house. Then he stopped and confronted her. It was strange. They had barely spoken for weeks – no, months – and yet it did not matter. All the old closeness was still there. Tom was glad. 'What's the matter?' he asked. 'Has something gone wrong, Mel?'

'No, but I think it's going to ... Tom, I'm really worried. I've got to stop our Darren. And your Jason's in it, too.'

'*In what?*'

Melanie shivered. The autumn night was clear but cold, and she sensed winter in the breeze. For a few seconds she did not speak. '*Come on*, Mel,' he repeated. 'What's happening?'

Quickly she told him what she had heard, missing no detail – and then repeated what her father had said earlier about the new threat of vandalism, and how it would destroy much more than mere machinery.

Tom nodded. 'He's dead right,' he said, looking down at Melanie's worried face, pale and yellow in the lamplight. 'The great daft idiots – do you think they've done it before, Mel?'

For some reason Melanie felt sure. 'No,' she said decisively. 'Something about the way they were talking ... I'm sure it's their first go. I think they're just copying what they've read about. What shall we do, Tom?'

'We *ought* to go in and tell my dad,' he said thoughtfully.

'No!' she said loudly. 'He'll tell the police.'

'No he won't, he's not a grass,' retorted Tom angrily.

They looked at each other for a few seconds – disappointed. Then Melanie said in a quiet, serious voice, 'Tom, we've got to stop them. It's my brother, and it's Lee's brother and it's your brother – and you don't want them to end up in prison any more than I do. We've *got* to think of a plan!'

Tom breathed deeply, thinking fast. 'You're right,' he said at last. 'But it won't be very easy to stop them without getting into trouble ourselves. Are you game?'

She nodded.

'OK, then,' said Tom. 'Now let's both think seriously about tactics . . .'

CHAPTER TWELVE

Just over an hour later Melanie stood silently in a shop doorway, watching the entrance to the Red Lion. A huge yellow moon, almost full, hung over the roofs, and stars sprinkled the sky. It was a beautiful night. But Melanie knew that her brother and his friends would not notice it; worse, they would not stop to think that on a clear night you can see everything that moves across the fields.

At last she saw them come out of the pub. Darren, Jason and Pete, and another man she did not know, turned right, and stood for a moment on the corner. They all wore heavy jackets, and looked oddly bulky and cumbersome, because of the tools they had strapped beneath their clothes. Darren carried a smallish red plastic container. Melanie watched them. Perhaps they had changed their minds. But no – they crossed the road, and began walking slowly in the direction of the colliery.

For a moment she watched, her eyes fixed on her brother in disbelief, as if the others were not there. Darren *loved* being a miner; he loved the jokiness of his mates at the coal face, and never minded the back-breaking work, or the dirt. He *loved* the pit. So how could he walk towards it now, to burn and destroy?

And what if someone got hurt by accident – badly hurt? He was her brother, but for a wild moment Melanie felt she did not know that clumsy, misshapen figure on the road ahead.

Shaking herself free of such thoughts, she darted after them, moving silently in her trainers, and was just a couple of yards behind when she cried out, 'Darren! Darren!'

Her brother stopped and looked round, astonished. She heard him swear quietly as he glanced at the others.

'Melanie – what are *you* doing out?'

This part of the plan was Melanie's idea. She had always enjoyed drama lessons in school, and this was one of her best performances. She panted as if she had been running for ages. 'Oh . . . Darren,' she puffed, 'it's these boys . . . they've been after me . . .'

'What boys?'

'Some lads, down the other end of the street . . . I was going to my friend's and they . . . they jumped out on me. It was horrible! They were – getting hold of me, and that.' She made her voice sound upset, even close to tears. For Melanie knew that no matter how distant he had become, nothing would stop Darren Wall from trying to look after his little sister.

'Who were they?' Her brother sounded angry, as she knew he would.

'I'm . . . I'm not sure. I think they were from Mexton,' she panted.

'Come on, Darren,' said Jason Farrell.

'Hang on, hang on – have they gone now, Mel?'

'No . . . no, they're *waiting* for me. At least, they were. Oh, Darren, I don't want to go back on my own. Can't you all come and see them off?' She clutched her brother's arm.

Darren hesitated, and looked at the others. 'What about it, then?'

'She's *your* sister, Wallsie,' said Jason, 'and I thought we had work to do.'

'How many of them were there?' asked Darren.

'Oh, about three,' mumbled Melanie, feeling terrible.

Pete Douglas laughed with the others. 'OK then, Darren, you think you can handle three little lads on your own?'

''Course I can,' growled Darren. He looked confused and bad-tempered. 'You go on. I can't ... I can't leave her by herself. I'll sort this out and catch you up – maybe. If I can. In any case ...'

'What?' said Jason.

'Since we couldn't get any more, to cause the diversion like ... maybe we should wait ...?'

Jason's voice was cold. 'I'm not stopping now, Wallsie.'

Melanie's heart sank. This was just what Tom had said would happen. She had thought they would all come with her, and she would take them on a fruitless search around Mainthorpe, by which time her parents would probably be walking down the road from the Club, and somehow the lads would have changed their minds. It was not going to work that way. Thank goodness Tom was out there waiting, ready to put the emergency plan into action.

Fifteen minutes later she was still walking around Mainthorpe with a brother who was becoming more and more irritated. 'How many of these lads did you say there were?'

'Five.'

'No, you didn't. You said three. What's going on, Melanie – have you been dreaming?'

'No, Darren! They were down there, and one of them bruised my arm.'

'Let's see, then.'

'Well ... the bruise won't have come up yet.'

'What's that rip on your sleeve?' he asked, pointing to an old tear. Melanie was overjoyed. 'Yes!' she said, 'that's what they did. One of them tried to pull my jacket off me, but I managed to stop him.' She knew she was sounding less and less convincing. But it did not matter. She had got Darren away. Now it was up to Tom.

Tom wished he felt as sure about his bit of the plan as Melanie was about hers. She had told him exactly what the older boys had planned – about cutting across the fields from West Lane. Sure enough, as he crouched in the shadows of a small copse of trees on the edge of the Mexton Road, he saw the three figures walk along, and noticed that Darren was not with them. His heart was beating faster than normal. It was a long walk to the pit. It would take them some time if they went the normal way, but that would be too dangerous. Tom guessed they would turn off soon and start to make a short-cut – and he was right. The three figures slid off the road, which glittered grey and empty in the moonlight.

Tom had worked out that there was only one thing to do. Melanie had told him exactly what she had heard, and he knew the geography of the colliery. He was convinced that they would not be so stupid as to go ahead – no matter how determined they were – if they saw that there were policemen patrolling the whole of the pit boundary. Yet he had already checked and found this was not the case. The police reinforcements had come, but were all in the van parked at the main gate. The usual policemen were on duty there too, standing watching the small handful of pickets who stood in front of their brazier.

As far as Jason's plot went, it was a perfect opportunity. If the lads were silent, they would probably succeed. But after that? Of course they would get caught in the end; they had to be stopped. Tom knew that somehow the police had to be drawn on – alerted in advance, so that they moved to patrol the whole of the perimeter fence. But how to do that – short of going and telling them that something was about to happen, when they would wait to catch the culprits red-handed?

Tom was the best runner in his year, and he had never run faster. Ahead of them already, he knew the little lanes and fields around Mainthorpe Colliery as well as he knew the hills further off – and now he was grateful for the hours he had spent exploring with his dad when he was younger. He was as quick and as silent as a fox, knowing every gap in the hedges, and not minding barbed wire that tore him as he ran.

At last, the pit was looming over him. He approached the high wire fence, his breath sounding unnaturally loud. He bent, picked up a large stone, and hurled it over the fence with all his force, so that it landed with a *clunk* somewhere inside the colliery. Then he crouched beneath a group of bushes, and waited.

He had counted on the noise travelling, and one of the policemen being sent by the sergeant to see what was happening – and he was right. So Tom threw another stone; this one skittered off the roof of one of the buildings. Then he turned and darted through the low bushes that grew all round the pit boundary. He made no attempt to be particularly quiet; in fact, he was careful to twang the metal of the fence from time to time – to be sure they knew someone was there. His idea was to lead a couple of policemen all around the perimeter fence, so that Jason, Pete and the other man would see that their plan was hopeless. Once the alarm was truly raised, he knew he could slip away easily.

Tom heard the footsteps behind getting closer. A

torch was flashing, although there was hardly need of it. Head down, he felt like a small hunted creature, dashing for its life – although of course (he told himself) he had no reason to be scared. No one could hurt him, and he wasn't doing any harm. All he had to do now was be more cunning than ever, and get away.

He no longer thought about the three would-be vandals – who, at that very moment, were hesitating in the shadow of a tree. They saw from afar the sudden movement of torches, and heard a shout. 'The place is crawling with coppers,' Jason hissed to the others. 'Looks like someone's tipped them off.' They stood, dejected suddenly after the excitement, weighed down by their tools. 'Come on, it's a waste of time,' said Pete Douglas. But Jason stood staring keenly in the bright moonlight.

Running head-down, Tom felt frightened now. He realized he had passed the dark area behind the canteen, where Darren had planned to cut their entry. He could hear the shouts of policemen and the crackle of their radios, coming closer. The thing to do, he calculated rapidly, was head for the little stream that bisected the field, and hide beneath the banks. Then they would realize it had been a false alarm, all would be quiet again, and he could make his escape.

Just then the moon disappeared behind a cloud, and darkness shuttered down all around. Panting, Tom allowed himself to stop for a half a second, and bent double to relieve the stitch in his side. Then he turned sharply at right angles, ready to run out across the field under cover of the welcome darkness . . .

Crash!

Tom felt that there was no air left for him to breathe. Winded, he rolled on the ground, feeling soil ram up into his mouth and nostrils.

'Got him, the . . .' The swear word was lost in

grunts. One set of hands tried roughly to pull him to his feet, while someone else gave him a thump in the ribs. He heard the tearing of his jacket, and cried out as a man's hand grasped his hair, pulling his head back. A torch was shone in his face.

'It's just a poxy kid!'

'Still a bleeding vandal, ain't he?'

The accents of the two policemen were not local. They came from further down south – and realizing that fact made Tom afraid. What would they do to him? The faces he could make out beyond the torch beam were hard and unfriendly.

'What do you think you're up to, hey?' asked one, pulling Tom's head back still further, so that a sharp pain licked his scalp.

Then a third policeman joined the other two, and Tom was overjoyed to hear an accent he recognized. 'Why, it's young Tom Farrell,' it said, 'Dunno for the life of me what he's doing out here.'

'Looking for trouble, I'd say,' said the first policeman, letting go of Tom's hair. His neck ached now, with the strain.

'No way!' said Mick Golding. 'This lad's dad – he's the leader of the working miners. Tom wouldn't cause no trouble.'

'Then what's he doing out here, then?'

'Well, Tom?' Mick Golding's voice was kind, but Tom said nothing.

'Come on, lad – it'll be worse if you don't let on.'

'I was just out for a walk,' mumbled Tom, avoiding the policeman's eyes.

He heard Mick Golding sigh, then click his tongue. 'Look,' he said to the others, 'you can't tell, but I'd put money on this lad – that he's straight. I'll tell you what, we've got enough trouble . . . so why don't I take him home and get his father to sort him out?'

The other policemen were reluctant at first, but the

thought of the warm van and the waiting card game persuaded them. So Tom was marched all the way home, his head aching, and blood from the cut on his face trickling into his mouth.

When Tony Farrell opened the front door a look of panic crossed his face at first. There was his son, jacket torn, blood mixed with dirt streaking his face ... Mr Farrell was sure there had been an accident. But when Mick Golding asked if he could step inside and explain, and when the young policeman had finished the story, looking with exasperation at his silent prisoner – then Tony Farrell began to look angry.

'I'm asking you again, Tom – what were you doing?'

'Nothing.'

'We thought he was a vandal,' said Mick. 'There's been a lot of it about.'

'Why would our Tom do anything like that?' said Tony Farrell derisively. 'He wouldn't even think of it, would you, lad?'

Still Tom said nothing at all. Whatever he told them would get someone into trouble, and so he knew he had to stay silent.

'I'd better get back on duty, then,' said Mick Golding with regret.

'You leave this lad to me,' said Tony meaningfully, glaring at Tom. Mrs Farrell offered the policeman a cup of tea, and he sipped it quickly, talking briefly to Mr Farrell about the strike.

'Mainthorpe's not what it was,' he murmured, 'and me – I've had enough. Some of the things I've seen – on both sides – well, it's sickened me, it has. I'm looking for something else now, out of the Force.'

'Don't blame you, mate,' said Tom's father.

Then at last both parents stood in the living room in front of their son.

'Tom!' said Mr Farrell. 'No lad of mine goes skulking around where he shouldn't be, causing trouble, without me knowing why. Now I'm giving you one more chance to tell me the truth . . .'

'I can't, Dad!'

Tom's mother frowned. 'It's something to do with that Melanie Wall, I bet,' she said, guessing – and Tom went crimson immediately. 'I thought so,' she said triumphantly. 'When whoever it was came to the door and you rushed off. It was a girl's voice – I heard it. That's my woman's instinct, that is, Tom! You ought to know better, after what we were saying to you.'

Tony Farrell chimed in, 'Her father's the biggest troublemaker in Mainthorpe, and she takes after him – as like as not.'

'No, she doesn't! You leave her out of it!' shouted Tom.

At that, his father's face changed. He looked knowing, and terribly disappointed. 'All right, Tom, you've answered us, in a way. I don't know what you've been up to, but all I can say is, if that girl's persuaded you on to *their* side, and if you've been up to no good, then I'll find out and I'll take my belt to you. And that I've never done in your whole life, have I?'

Tom looked at his father, and shook his head, his eyes filling with tears. He could not bear it that his father thought he had been doing something bad, or planning to . . . and yet how could he explain? They would only hate Melanie for dragging him into trouble, even if it was for the right reasons.

Then a strange thought struck him. What if he told the truth, and it turned out that his father would have *wanted* Darren and all of them to go ahead – because of the bad publicity for the strike? Even Jason, too – because his father still would not speak to his older son, or have him in the house.

Tom reflected bitterly that six months ago he would

have been incapable of thinking anything so cynical. But that was what the strike had done – it had made them all change. It had made them all harder. Anyway, it was too late to explain now. Even if they approved what he had done (which was unlikely) he had made a choice when he left the house to join Melanie in the street. He had moved away from them – into the cold, where you had to grow up, on your own.

His father sighed. Tom's heart ached at the grief and disappointment in his face. 'Get to bed, lad. *My* father would have taken a belt to you already, but that's not my way. Still, you'll not go out until I get to the bottom of this, you hear me?'

Without another word, Tom turned and left the room. At the bottom of the stairs he paused, something catching his eye. Lying on the doormat was a crumpled piece of paper that had not been there before. He bent to pick it up, and smoothed it a little. He knew the handwriting – large and clumsy as it was.

TOM – I KNOW IT WAS YOU. I SAW YOU RUNNING TO TIP THEM OFF. MY OWN BROTHER IS A GRASS. WE WON'T FORGET WHAT YOU DONE.

Tom stared at the words in disbelief. Then, hearing his parents moving to the living room door, he quickly crumpled the note and shoved it roughly in his pocket.

CHAPTER THIRTEEN

Tom checked the ring, then watched the pigeon whirl into the air with a juddering motion. The rest cooed and rustled inside their shed. He kept his eyes on the speck in the sky – funny how different this was from watching a wild thing like a hawk. You knew the bird would come home. That was certain – as certain as the fact that you yourself would always come home. Home. But where *was* home? Where your family is, Tom supposed. But what happened when other people became like family – when you were married, for instance? He sighed. That must be difficult to work out.

Now Jason was no longer at home, and Jason obviously hated him. And Mum and Dad no longer thought of this little house, that they had done up so carefully, as home – because they wanted to leave it. And something else occurred to Tom: his dad hadn't mentioned the pigeons when he talked of moving. Did people keep pigeons down south?

He went into the shed, reached for another bird, and let that one heave itself into the sky as well. They needed their exercise, these little feathered prisoners – but they would not want to be let loose in the wide world. And nor did Tom.

It was two days since his escapade at the colliery, and still his parents were cool with him. It was unusual. They said nothing more about Lord Grafton's job offer, but it was in the air — as if written in large letters on the living room wall. Linda had begun packing her toys into a cardboard box, until Tom told her not to be silly. All those shouts and screams on the way to school ... little Linda had finished with Mainthorpe, too.

It was only Tom ... and he could not quite understand what was going on in his own mind. There was the question of belonging. Your accent, for example. He remembered the way the girl Rosie had spoken at the prize giving, and it made him squirm — not because there was anything wrong with it, but because it was so different. But that was daft too. What did it matter how you spoke? The trouble was — he thought that people who spoke poshly did not understand those who didn't. And maybe it worked the other way too.

What would he say to his parents? He could not believe that they were waiting for his decision on the move, yet his dad had said so. And he always meant — and did — what he said.

'Hey up, Tom.' Eddy Smith ambled into the back yard, hands deep in the pockets of his jeans, collar turned up against the slight drizzle on the wind. Tom nodded to him. Eddy was fine with him now; Lee was still sometimes distant. Tom knew that Lee's dad was still passionate about the strike, whereas Eddy's father had been thinking of going back to work.

'What shall we do?' asked Eddy.

'I can't do much. I'm not allowed out — because of the other night.'

Tom had told his friends what had happened, but not why. He said that he was simply wandering about, to see what it was like down by the pit at night. They believed him — and the fact that he had been caught by the police gave Tom a certain glamour to the other boys. 'Did they thump you?' they asked with relish. Yes, he told them truthfully. Then even boys who had not been friendly to him looked at him with admiration.

Eddy asked for a cup of tea. As he put the kettle on, Tom noticed that his friend looked worried.

'Oh, it's not much,' said Eddy. 'Just Dad.'

'What's up with him?'

'Well, he got a letter this morning. They're all getting it. From the Coal Board. It says they'll get extra money if they go back to work now. A sort of bonus.'

Tom whistled. 'A bribe, in other words.'

'I suppose so.'

'What did he say?'

'It's not what *he* said, it's what our mum said. She's been going on since eight o'clock this morning. Says she's fed up trying to make ends meet, and all that, and he should take it. She says we won't be able to have a proper Christmas if he don't.'

Eddy Smith was one of five children, and Tom knew that things had been really difficult for him at home. He had not talked about it much, but Tom thought he looked thinner and paler – as if none of them were getting the right sort of food to eat.

'So what's your dad say?'

'He lost his temper in the end, and told her to stop nagging. He says he'll make his own mind up. I think he'd like to go back, but he's afraid . . . not of anybody, I mean. But of giving up. After all this time.'

Tom nodded. He understood that. It was like doing cross-country running, and you had a stitch but knew you were near the end of the course. And so you forced yourself to carry on, no matter what it cost you, no matter how great the pain. This strike was like that – a punishing cross country marathon in weather that got worse all the time.

'Hasn't *your* dad said anything about it?' asked Eddy.

Tom shook his head.

'That's funny, I'd have thought he would. Because yesterday he made a big speech telling them that they ought to accept. My dad says he were shouted down.'

Tom groaned. 'Oh no, more trouble,' he said. 'They'll be coming round here and breaking the windows one of these nights.'

Eddy nodded. 'It's a lot of money on offer,' he said.

'What do *you* think?' Tom asked.

Eddy shrugged. 'Oh, I dunno. I suppose I'd rather he went back, if it didn't seem . . . I'm sick of having nowt in my pockets, and Mum being so miserable all the time, and the whole thing.'

'Ay,' said Tom. And the boys sat in silence for a while, cradling the hot mugs.

Meanwhile Melanie was enjoying herself. The Women's Group's soup kitchens were a great success; half the kids in Mainthorpe thought of them as a social club as much as a place to get food. The atmosphere in the hall was jolly, almost like a party at times. Little children raced around, pushing toys that jangled and beeped. Women sat talking and laughing. There was a delicious smell of hot soup, as the thick liquid, full of vegetables, was ladled into plastic bowls.

Melanie was on ladle duty – with another girl her age, and two of her mother's friends. They stood at a long trestle table at one end of the hall. She ripped open another large sliced loaf, and gave two slices to the small boy who held out his hand. It made her feel important – completely grownup.

'Good, isn't it, love?'

Her mother stood behind her, surveying the hall. Melanie nodded. 'Ay, it's the nicest yet. Must be the tomatoes in it.'

'No, I don't mean the soup! I mean all this.' Mrs Wall waved a hand in the air – taking in the benches, the soup, the children, the smiling women and the men who were talking over their cigarettes. 'It's like folk weren't together before – not really. We thought we were, but we were all in our little houses watching the television. Now we're really together. And us women – we'll never be the same again, Mel.'

'Why?' Melanie loved her mother's face when it wore this shining look. She knew what the answer would be, but she loved to hear it said again and again.

'We know how to organize ourselves now! We won't be happy to stay at home in the kitchen when all this is over!'

Melanie knew it was true. Her mother had changed so much. She was about to say so, when she noticed Jason Farrell making his way across the hall towards her. She grabbed a plastic bowl, and filled it with soup, and hoped that he would not speak to her. In any case, she thought, he could not say much in front of her mother. But as bad luck would have it, Mrs Wall chose just that moment to spot someone she wanted to talk to, and move away.

Jason nodded at her, unsmiling. She held out the bowl of soup to him, and yet he did not move away. He stood there for a few seconds, lifting spoonfuls of the soup to his mouth, never taking his eyes off her face.

'You seen my brother then?' he said at last.

''Course I have, at school.'

'That's not what I mean, and you know it,' he interrupted. 'Somebody tells me you were seen hanging round outside the Red Lion the other night, when a certain lad got caught by the pit. And a certain Darren Wall tells me he found no strange lads in Mainthorpe attacking his precious little sister. Funny, isn't it?'

'Oh yeah, I can't stop laughing,' Melanie retorted.

'I may be as thick as two short planks but I can work some things out. You heard us and Darren talking about something, and you went along and told my precious brother, who went and grassed on us to the cops.'

'He didn't! He got caught by the police, and one of them thumped him!' cried Melanie. Then she looked nervously around, to see if people were listening.

'Oh yeah!' jeered Jason, disbelievingly. 'So in that case, what was he doing out there at all? Looking for owls? Practising his boy scout whistles?' He laughed – an ugly, mocking sound.

'How do you know he wasn't?' asked Melanie furiously. 'You don't know anything about your brother, Jason Wall!'

'Oh, I *do*. I know plenty about him,' he replied, looking at her with contempt. And then he sauntered away, leaving Melanie feeling that all the jollity in the hall had melted away. She put down the ladle and told one of the women that she was going outside.

She leaned against the wall and looked down the street. The windows of the primary school opposite were decorated with cut-outs of witches and black cats. And then Melanie remembered. It was Hallowe'en. On Mischief Night all the little kids of the village would go out 'mischieving' – rattling letterboxes and tapping on windows. Hollowed-out turnips with carved faces would be put in windows, candles glowing inside them. The night would be filled with fun, fright and naughtiness. Melanie used to love it. But now, she reflected, she was too old to go out mischieving. That was what was terrible about growing up. One minute you liked to feel like an adult, serving soup to people; the next minute you wished you were nine or ten and could still play with toys and act silly on Hallowe'en.

That is – if they were allowed out this year. What

with all the police around the place, and the bad feelings between people because of the strike, the parents might keep their children indoors. 'It's more than witches that's scary,' Melanie said to herself, 'it's people – sometimes.'

'You OK, Mel?' It was Jackie.

'Ay, I was just thinking of how we used to go mischieving.'

Jackie smiled. 'Remember that time old Mrs Wainwright gave you a carrot, 'cos sweets are bad for you, she said?'

Melanie smiled back. 'I wish I was a little kid again.'

'Me too,' said Jackie – and the two friends leaned against the wall in silence, thinking of the past.

Then they noticed two figures coming along the road towards them. Jackie glanced at Melanie. 'It's Tom and Eddy,' she said.

Tom felt like a prisoner suddenly granted freedom. His parents had relented and said that he could go out with Eddy; he'd grabbed his money and disappeared before they could change their minds.

The boys drew near, and Jackie waved at them. Since the story of Tom's 'arrest' had gone around the school (being exaggerated all the time, so that in the end he had fought with six policemen) she had been rather admiring of him.

'Hey up, you two,' she called. 'Where you off to?'

'We're getting the bus to Doncaster to look around,' said Tom, adding on impulse, 'Why don't you two come with us?'

Jackie pulled a face. 'No bus fare,' she said gloomily.

Tom was glad of his hoarded prize money. 'I've got enough for us all,' he said enthusiastically. 'Oh, go on.'

'I'll go and ask Mum,' said Melanie excitedly, dashing inside.

'No one to ask at home,' said Jackie, with some relief in her voice. 'They're all at Auntie Beryl's.'

Mrs Wall frowned for just a second at the request, but then her face cleared. She was in a good mood. 'Just don't tell your dad,' was all she said, and Melanie felt that the two of them were friends, conspirators even.

So less than an hour later the four got off the bus, chattering happily, and not minding the drizzle. The town centre was crowded, the shop windows bright and enticing. They spent ages in the record shop, flicking through the albums, and listening to the tracks that were blaring out.

They tried to run the wrong way up an escalator and were told off by a shop assistant. Then they looked in the trendiest teenage clothes shops, and Tom tried on a leather jacket. While Eddy was not listening, Melanie told him he looked really good in it, and Jackie teased him for going bright red.

Doncaster had never seemed so exciting to Melanie. The four of them laughed a lot, and she knew that sometimes they must have sounded like eleven year olds – but it did not matter. What mattered was being friends, and having fun, and being away from all the strains of Mainthorpe – just for a while.

Tom bought them all hot dogs from a street stall, and they munched contentedly, tomato sauce smearing their cheeks. 'Ohh, this is lovely,' sighed Melanie, 'I wish we didn't have to go back.'

But of course they did. The bus pulled past wet pavements glittering with reflections. Shops were closing; Melanie watched people hurrying home, laden with shopping. She settled contentedly back in her seat, happier than she had been for ages. Jackie sat next to her, while the boys sat in front, Eddy reading a pop magazine.

Melanie tapped Tom on the shoulder. 'Do you

think witches'll fly out tonight?' she asked, jerking her head out at the darkness. They had left the town now, and were bowling along an open road. 'I used to get really scared when I went to bed on Hallowe'en.'

'So did I,' said Tom. 'Once I thought I heard a witch cackling in the corner of my bedroom. Jason was downstairs, so I was on my own. I screamed for our mum, and it turned out to be a shiny paper bag that was crumpled in the waste paper basket.'

Jackie joined in Melanie's laughter. Then she asked, 'Yes, but, do you *believe* in them, Tom? In witches and ghosts and things like that – bad things? What about you, Mel?'

Melanie thought. 'Sometimes I think I do, because you can't tell what's flying about in the night, can you? And you can't *prove* they're not real.'

'Oh, I'm sure bad things are real enough,' said Tom. 'Only I think they walk about on two legs. I don't think they fly, or go through walls.'

'That's a relief,' said Melanie, shivering suddenly.

'Oh, I dunno,' he said slowly, 'I'm starting to think that those old pictures you see of the devil with horns and a tail, are just plain stupid. I wonder when people started to think that maybe he looks just like the man next door?'

Then, as if he could not bear the subject, Tom made his free hand into a claw and made it crawl along the back of the seat. The girls leaned on each other, giggling – making the people across the aisle look across at them and smile.

Eddy looked up from his reading to grin, too. But despite all the laughter, despite the lovely afternoon, Tom felt . . . oh, it was hard to explain, even to himself. A sort of sense of *ending* – that was it. That nothing would ever be so good again.

CHAPTER FOURTEEN

On Sunday morning, Tom woke early. He had slept well, his dreams disturbed by no dark images. Usually he would lie in until ten or eleven o'clock, or until his father came knocking at the bedroom door and insisting he get up. He stretched, wondering why he felt so wide awake. Then he put his arms behind his head, and grinned up at the ceiling, thinking of yesterday afternoon. Such fun, it had been. Perfect.

He could hear sounds from the kitchen, the rattle of pans, and the soft sound of his mother's voice. Linda raced past his bedroom door. His father called up to her, doors opened and closed, the radio was switched on ... All the usual comforting, homely Sunday morning sounds, which gave a pattern to life. Tom liked lying there listening, but this morning he felt full of energy. And so he heaved himself out of bed, and before long was bounding down the stairs – to his parents' astonishment.

'You're up early, lad! Is something wrong?' Mr Farrell looked cheerful. Tom immediately felt guilty that he had said nothing about the move. Today – he would speak today. He would tell them about yesterday, and how happy he had been with his friends. He would tell them that they must stay in Mainthorpe, because he was doing well at the Ernest Bevin and a move to a new school might set him back in his work. He would tell them that the strike would soon be over, and life in Mainthorpe would be back to normal. Yes – thought Tom happily – he would *tell* them.

Mrs Farrell hummed along with the radio, as she handed him a bowl of porridge. After eating it quickly, Tom bent to unbolt the back door. Opening it, he smiled. It was a lovely crisp, clear morning. Deep orange and brown leaves blazed against the delicate blue sky. It was a beautiful sight and made Tom feel more light-hearted than ever.

'Close the door, Tom, you're letting in the cold,' protested his mother.

'Just going out to look at the birds,' Tom called over his shoulder, doing as she asked.

Tony Farrell was deep in his newspaper, and Tom's mother knew better than to talk to him. She sat drinking her tea for a few minutes, then absent-mindedly switched off the radio as she went to go upstairs to make the beds. The kitchen was quiet for a while. Then Tom's father looked up, noticing the silence, and rose to switch on the sound once more.

It was then that he glanced out of the kitchen window, and saw something that made his hand fall away from the radio. At the bottom of the yard, the door of the pigeon hut was open. There was nothing particularly strange about that, but there was about Tom. The boy was *kneeling* in the small doorway, his head bent, in a sort of crouch. He looked as if he might be saying his prayers, or else bending to pick up something broken from the floor. Mr Farrell frowned, puzzled.

Then the still, Sunday-morning air was split by an anguished wail: 'Dad! Dad! *Daaaaa-ad!*' The sound was not so much a cry, as a roar – like that of a wounded animal. Tony Farrell tore open the back door, and was across the yard in a couple of strides.

Tom heard his father's footsteps, and turned round. His face was white, and he was holding something.

'*Dad!*' he whispered desperately. '*Just look!*'

A bird flopped in his outstretched hand. The feathers were mottled beautiful blue-pink and grey, but the little eyes were filmed over, and the head lolled crazily on its broken neck. A few wisps of down rose into the air inside the hut, caught in a draught from the open door. They floated above a scene of destruction. For there on the floor lay the other birds – all seven of them thrown down carelessly in a heap of ruffled feathers which still had the beautiful gleam of life, although all the necks flopped uselessly.

Mr Farrell did not speak, and nor did his son. They stared at the terrible scene with disbelief. Tony Farrell went to pick up one of the birds to see if it might be alive, then stopped. There was no point.

'Oh God,' he said at last, in a choked voice. 'God! But who . . . who would . . .?'

'Lots of people, Dad,' said Tom bitterly.

At that, he began to cry. He had been holding it back since the moment before he had opened the door, and knew in that second – because of the dead silence inside – that something was wrong. Now he carefully and lovingly laid down the pigeon he had been holding, and saw in that little heap of dead bodies a flashing image of how they once had been. Beautiful. Cooing gently to greet him. Whirling into the air with a purple-blue sheen on their wings. Juddering down again, returning home as they were trained to do. All gone. All over.

Still kneeling there, he sobbed with great racking cries, for the pigeons who had not harmed anyone. They had been punished by human beings – murdered when they were innocent of all the crimes that men committed. They had been punished because of what Tony Farrell had done. Or maybe even – because of what Tom had done.

Always the relentless drumbeat, '*Who? Who? Who?*' hammered in Tom's brain . . .

Jason. Surely he would never . . . and yet he wanted to get his own back for the other night, he had written it in that note. He of all people would know how easy it was to get over the back yard wall, and understand just how important the pigeons were to the Farrells. A part of Tom's brain reasoned that any man who resented Tony Farrell's speech at the last meeting could have done this. Still his heart thudded out the horrible reply that it was Jason's revenge.

'I d-don't understand it, T-Tom, I j-just don't understand it . . .' his father stammered, as if trying to control his own tears. 'I never would have thought that *anyone* would do a thing like that. N-not anyone . . .'

Tom felt his father's hands pull him very gently to his feet, and they stood together at that sad doorway, staring into the silent hut. Then Tom looked at his father with a face that was streaked with dirt and tears, a face that was tense with pain.

'Dad!' he whispered, 'let's get out of here. Let's go and live down south like you want to. I don't want to stay here with all those people who hate us. Who'd do this . . . We've got to get away from here. We've *got* to leave.'

CHAPTER FIFTEEN

For a week Tom refused to go to school. His parents were helpless; they saw the rage and grief on his face, and left him alone.

'The lad'll get over it,' said Mrs Farrell, leaning over the ironing board and wishing that what she said would come true.

'No, he won't,' replied Tom's father. 'He'll never forget it. Some things, you don't.'

That was what Tom thought too. He closed his eyes and pictured the feathered bodies, and remembered the soft plopping sound each one made as they threw them into the deep hole dug where the hut had been. The pile of firewood in the corner of the yard was now the only sign that there had ever been a hut full of cooing birds. But Tom knew he would always remember them – always.

And of course, it was more than the birds. Deep down he knew that something had happened to him that morning that would stay with him for the rest of his life. It was a sad and terrible thing, but there was nothing he could do about it. Some people probably grew up without ever finding out the truth about human beings, Tom thought – and they were lucky. But for him the year in which he became fourteen would always be associated with his discovery that people could hate as much as *that*.

After a week he knew he must go back to school, and came down for breakfast at his normal time. His parents exchanged secret looks of relief. Already the atmosphere in the house was lighter because the decision had been taken. But Tom resented the fact that his father seemed to have got over the loss of the pigeons so quickly. 'He didn't care about them as much as I did,' he thought. And that made him feel more isolated than ever.

But in the yard before school began, a strange thing happened. Tom stood alone as he always did, but people waved casually to him, and boys went out of their way to walk near and say 'All right?' Tom smiled grimly to himself. They all knew, and they were sorry – were they? Well, it was too late. In his new mood it seemed quite easy for him to imagine turning the tables. Once he had been sent to Coventry; now he would send the whole of them to Coventry . . .

Suddenly Melanie was standing in front of him. For a few moments she was silent, as if searching for the right thing to say. Then she touched his arm, and whispered, 'I heard about . . . oh, Tom, I'm so sorry.'

He looked at her coolly. 'Why? Did you do it?'

She flushed, as if someone had slapped her. 'Don't be like that.'

'Why?'

'Because . . . because it's not my fault, Tom. You know that.'

He looked down at her, with an expression she had never seen before – something cold and hostile. 'I reckon I don't know anything, Melanie – not any-more. Except that it's *easy* for people to say things aren't their fault. It's easy to pretend to be friends, when all the time you know which side you're on.'

'I thought we didn't believe in all that – not any-more?' said Melanie, in a small voice.

'No choice, is there?' he replied shortly.

She could feel anger well up in her, but tried to keep it down – tried to understand his unfairness. 'Listen, Tom,' she said, 'it's no good being like this to me. I'd do anything to bring your birds back to life, but there's nothing I can do, is there? And I hate whoever it was that killed them . . .'

'Do you? Well what if it was your brother, and mine? You wouldn't hate your Darren, would you? Course you wouldn't – because in the end, he's on your side – and it was people from your side killed my birds. And that's all there is to it.' With that he turned and walked away.

Melanie stood and watched Tom's departing back, until the swing doors had closed on him. All her anger had evaporated; there were tears in her eyes. Tom was being unfair, but she understood why – and just wanted to cry for the pain she saw in his eyes. But she couldn't reach him – or at least, not yet. Melanie heard the bell clang, and Jackie calling, so she threw back her head and tried to fix a normal expression on her face. Whatever happened, she knew that Tom would be her friend again. One day he would make a move to jump the great, deep chasm between them.

Christmas decorations started to appear in the streets of Doncaster ('Too early, as usual,' Mrs Wall complained) and the pressure on the striking miners grew and grew. They were tempted to return to work, for Christmas would be cheerless with no pay packets. It was worse for the parents with small children, who watched the television advertisements and asked their mothers for toys they could not possibly have. Not this year.

The bonus the men were offered was a good one: an

'incentive', the newspapers called it. 'More like black-mail,' snorted Mr Wall. Some men took it. Most didn't.

At last Jim Wall's case came up before the Magistrate's Court, and he was fined £300 for obstructing the police. That made him laugh. 'Where am I supposed to find that kind of money? By applying to the Coal Board, I suppose!' Secretly, Melanie was disappointed that he hadn't gone to prison – oh, just for a few days of course. Another man had been sentenced to a month, which would have been terrible. But she had imagined going to visit him, and it had seemed romantic – like many old films she had seen on the television.

She knew the thought was wrong, that it was *silly*. But she could not help it. Many things were wrong, and sometimes it surprised Melanie how you could know that and yet get used to them. One day she walked past the Golding's house, and saw that someone had sprayed the words **'POLICE SCAB'** on the walls of the little house. It looked horrible. Four days later she heard her mother tell her father that Angie Golding had left, taking Rob home to her mother. 'She couldn't stand the strain,' said Susan Wall, with a note of pity in her voice.

'The rest of us have to stand it,' said her husband with a shrug.

Melanie saw her mother glance at him reproachfully. 'That's all very well, Jim,' she said, 'but there's lots of marriages already broken up in Mainthorpe because of the strike. It's not easy for people, you know.'

'I never said it was,' he replied shortly.

Why, wondered Melanie, over and over again, *have people changed so much*? There was the time when Mick Golding and a young policewoman were chased and cornered in an alley by a crowd of men, and would have been badly beaten if it hadn't been for the timely arrival of a squad car. It was in all the papers. It shocked Melanie, but not her parents. 'But he's your *cousin*, Mum. And that policewoman was only a young girl, and she was from round here. How could they . . .?' Melanie protested. Her mother just shrugged. 'They're police,' was all she said.

At other times Melanie understood that resentment completely. Five men were arrested for picking coal from the heap near the pit. It was very cold now; the men had no money; they needed that coal for their families. How could that be a crime? It wasn't, said Mr and Mrs Wall, angrily. Would they let families shiver rather than turn a blind eye to them picking up some waste coal nobody wanted? The answer was hard and horrible: *yes, they would, in this war*. Realising that, Melanie felt harder herself. She hated the police who had arrested those men, and knew which side she was on.

She began to dream, tossing and turning in her little bed so that old Fred always fell to the floor, unable to comfort her any more. And in her dreams she was bending to pick coal on a heap that was moving, sliding dangerously, and then she was being chased across its treacherous surface, running in terror to avoid arrest . . . until she found that the ground had hardened under her feet, and she was running down a dark alley, panting, hearing the pounding footsteps draw nearer and nearer. And then there was the high brick wall at the end, no exit, no escape, only the necessity of turning to face the angry faces, who jeered at the policewoman's uniform which, suddenly, she was wearing. Always angry shouts echoed in Melanie's dreams – screams of abuse one side hurled at the other, so that Melanie, like the piggy-in-the-middle, ducked and covered her head, in case the words should land heavily upon her.

She only mentioned Tom Farrell's pigeons once at home, and the response was predictable. 'It's not very nice, love, but these things happen,' said her mother.

'*Why*, though?' Melanie asked helplessly.

'Because.' That was all her mother said.

'People get fed up, they want to hit back,' said her father.

'At *birds*?' said Melanie scornfully. Then she looked suspiciously at her brother. 'Did you know anything about it, Darren Wall?'

He looked up briefly from his paper. 'I know I didn't do it. And none of my mates did it either, Mel. If I want to hurt something, it'll be wearing a blue uniform, not bleeding feathers!'

One good thing had come from the killing of the pigeons. A week after Tom had returned to school there was a knock at the front door. Mr Farrell was watching television, and asked Tom to see who it was. Tom's mother was upstairs helping Linda get ready for bed.

Tom opened the door, then stepped backwards. 'Oh, it's you,' he said.

Jason stood squarely on the doorstep. Tom noticed that immediately; his brother rarely stood up straight, but lounged, or leaned – always looking as if he did not care much, as if he would shrug the world off with casual cheek. Now his thickset shoulders were back, and his legs were planted firmly apart – as if he had geared himself up to this, and had an announcement to make.

'Aye, it's me all right,' he said.

The two boys looked at each other in silence for a few minutes. Jason was the first to drop his eyes.

'I heard about the birds,' he said.

'Did you?'

'I did.'

'So?'

138

'So . . .'

As Jason hesitated, Tom felt anger rush up inside his chest. 'So – was that your way of getting your own back on me, Jason? *So* – what's it feel like to wring a bird's neck?'

Jason jerked his head up at that, and his cheeks were scarlet. 'I knew it,' he said. 'I knew you'd think it was me. Well, I'll tell you something for nothing. If I could find out who did that, if I could get my hands on him, he wouldn't walk home! If I . . .'. But he could not finish. The words choked.

Tom could not speak either. All he knew was that he was glad. He could tell that Jason was telling the truth, and the knowledge made something heal inside him, a wound that had hurt even more than the destruction of the birds. Jason had not done it. No resentment could be that cruel, not within *their* family. Jason had come to say so.

'Why don't you come in?' said Tom gruffly. 'Mum's upstairs with Linda. Give them a surprise.'

And Jason stepped over the threshold for the first time in months. As he passed Tom in the narrow hall he paused. 'What will Dad say?' he asked nervously – all the old bravado gone.

'I'll talk to him,' said Tom stoutly.

There were cries of delight from Linda's little bedroom, when the familiar feet, in their heavy work boots, clumped upstairs. Tom went into the living room, where his father was reading the paper. 'Our Jason's come back, Dad,' he said in a rush, 'and you said he shouldn't. But . . . he's sorry about the pigeons, and it wasn't him, he said so, and I think you should let him back now . . .' He faltered, for his father said nothing.

Anxiety showed in his mother's face too, as she came into the room and stood quietly at her husband's side. 'Our Jason's here, Tony,' she said, with a hint of questioning in her voice.

There was a silence. Then at last Mr Farrell raised his head and looked at her. 'Well, why don't you put the kettle on, love,' he said.

CHAPTER SIXTEEN

At last it was all over. Melanie came home from school and found her father sitting at the table, his head in his hands. When he looked up at her she thought (but could not be sure) that his eyes were wet. 'It's over, Mel,' he said hoarsely. 'They've sold us out.'

There was no mistaking the tears in her mother's eyes. 'All that struggle, for all those months,' she whispered, 'and now they've given in, they've betrayed us.'

The strike which had been thrown over Mainthorpe like a great blanket – smothering, but oddly comforting too – was suddenly taken away, leaving people blinking in the sudden cold. It had become familiar, almost necessary, that thing which had enveloped them all, and without it they had to look at their bleak, altered world – and ask *what was it all for?*

It was not, as Jim Wall said bitterly, up to the people of Mainthorpe. The leaders of the National Union said that the strike was over, and so over it was – and the men who had manned the picket lines at Mainthorpe had no choice but to stay home. 'I wouldn't mind,' said Mrs Wall, 'but we've got nothing out of it. They haven't got any agreement not to close pits. They've got nothing for us. And after all we've been through.'

That refrain was repeated again and again, as newspapers wrote encouraging the 'people in the mining communities' to forgive, forget, and go back to work. But it was not so easy. If anything, the sudden ending made both sides feel worse, each blaming the other for the whole thing. Some households in Mainthorpe were happy, others felt as angry and disappointed as the Walls. Some women smiled for the first time as they walked down the street, relishing the thought of a pay-packet coming into the house once more. Others kept their eyes down, beaten. 'And after all this *time*,' they said to each other, shaking their heads.

The Ernest Bevin Comprehensive was preparing for Christmas. The hall was decorated for the Christmas disco, and the windows of the lower school were festooned and stuck about with cotton wool and cut-tissue 'stained glass'. Nobody talked much about presents – although the fact that people all over the country had raised money for the Families of Miners Appeal, organized by the women, still amazed them. It would still be needed, because the return to work would not be until after Christmas – but everyone knew it had to be shared between many coalfields, many villages. 'At least there'll be roast chicken on Christmas Day,' said Lofty Lennard, smacking his lips.

He had taken to hanging around Melanie – much to Jackie's amusement. 'It's ever since that fight he's fancied you, Mel,' she giggled, 'cos he never thought a girl would take him on. Hasn't got over the shock!' Since *she* liked both Lofty's friends, Billy and Dave, she did not mind the boys loitering around the school gates and walking along with them.

Melanie didn't mind either. Tom spoke to her politely, as he did to everyone, but that was all. He was like a robot, she sometimes thought – and although it hurt her, she became used to it. And wasn't that the thing she had learnt, above everything else, that year? That you *did* get used to things, no matter how bad they were.

The kids responded to the news that the strike was over more or less as their parents had. Some of them were furious and said the Union had 'sold out'. Others were relieved. Some were so bored by the whole thing they did not care any more, and just looked forward to the disco.

Melanie felt confused about it – but then (she thought) she felt confused about everything these days. It must be to do with getting older – that everything seemed so complicated, and there were no easy answers. Not even to how you felt about this boy or that boy. She was flattered that Lofty liked her, and sometimes angry with Tom; yet Tom was her *friend*, she realised (even if he didn't realise it at the moment) and that was more important than any passing crush.

'But who will you go to the disco with, Mel?' asked Jackie.

'You, of course!' Melanie replied.

'I've got nothing to wear.'

'Nor have I.'

'My mum said I could alter her red jeans.'

And so the girls went on talking about the usual things. It was as if the strike had never happened.

At the Farrells' house china was being wrapped in newspapers and packed carefully into cardboard boxes. Tom's mother would let no one help; she dusted her wedding presents and laid them in the packing cases, glad that they would be on display in a new place. Tom had not seen his mother so happy or excited for a long time.

Yet the family had kept their imminent departure a

secret. The headmasters of both schools had been told, but even Linda had promised not to tell anyone they were going. 'Not until it's about to happen,' explained Linda, 'because we don't want people being nasty because they're jealous, do we?' She was nine now, and understood what nastiness was. The name 'Scab!' still rang in her ears.

Lord and Lady Grafton had sent them a photograph of their new home, and arranged all the details about schools, insurance, and so on. Tony Farrell was not a man to gush, but he was touched by their kindness, and knew his decision was right. Only one thing spoiled the family's quiet preparations: Jason said he would not come.

He had moved back home, just until they left, but then he was going back to live with the Douglasses. 'I've got a new girlfriend,' he explained shyly, 'from Mexton. And ... well, I know people here, and I've got the job ...'

'I understand, love,' said Mrs Farrell sadly, 'but won't you just come down until after Christmas?' Jason shook his head and looked away. He was independent now – moving out had given him that feeling, and he knew he could never return.

'You'll write?' asked his mother, and he nodded. But both of them knew that Jason was not much good at letters.

On the Saturday two weeks before Christmas, Melanie was woken by her mother, who put a cup of tea by her bed, and threw something down. 'Here's a letter for you, pet. Somebody must have shoved it through early this morning.'

Melanie yawned, rubbed the sleep from her eyes and sat up. The room was cold. She shivered and snuggled back down under the bedclothes, taking the small blue envelope with her. Clumsily, she ripped it open.

Dear Melanie,
I've got something I want to say to you, so
will you meet me today? I'll be up at the Slab
at 12, and I'll bring us some food. Hope you
can come. I'll wait.

> Tom

An hour later she was cycling along the road past
the pit, wearing as many layers of clothing as she
could, and with a woolly hat pulled well down over
her ears. It was crisp and clear, and the sun sparkled
on fields iced with frost. The brightness of the sky
made her screw up her eyes. It was beautiful. Though
Melanie was used to that landscape, she still caught
her breath when she noticed the curve of the hills all
round Mainthorpe Colliery. 'God rest you, Merry
Gentlemen, let nothing you dismay ...' she sang
loudly, her breath clouding on the cold air like
dragon's smoke.

The Slab was the name local people gave to a
rough, granite monument up on one of the hills over-
looking the pit. It had been erected in the thirties, as a
memorial to twenty-two men killed in an underground
explosion; sometimes people would leave little bunches
of flowers at its base, in memory of a father or grandfather whose name was carved on its dark, gritty surface.

When at last Melanie reached the memorial, puffing
with the effort of the climb, she saw that Tom was
already there, sitting on a black plastic dustbin sack,
eating a packet of crisps. Suddenly she felt shy, and
she could tell by his expression that he did, too.

'I'm glad you could come,' he said.

'You could have waited,' Melanie grinned, throwing
down a packet of chocolate biscuits.

'Sorry. I'm starved. Anyway, look what I brought
us.' He pointed to the large thermos flask that stood

upright against the old stone wall. 'Hot soup. Thick vegetable. We'll have to share the cup, though.'

'That's OK. You haven't got germs, have you?'

'Yeah, and they're flying to getcha ...' He made a face, and waggled his fingers at her, and she shrank back, laughing. It was just like before; he was the same silly Tom. And the strike was over, so everything could be like it was before ... The great rush of relief made Melanie want to laugh out loud.

For a while they busied themselves with eating; it covered the slight awkwardness of their reunion. Then at last Melanie asked, 'Well, what were you going to tell me?' He looked up, as if surprised, and she smiled. 'Your *note*, dummy! – you said you had something to tell me.'

'Oh ... ay. I did.'

Melanie laughed. '*Did?* Haven't you anymore?'

Then she stopped, staring at him. He was sitting, his hands clasped around his knees, avoiding her gaze.

'You look right serious, Tom,' she said.

'We're moving house,' he said shortly.

'Oh.'

He nodded. 'Was anything said in school?'

'Yes,' said Melanie slowly, 'but that was ages ago. It was only a rumour. I didn't believe it. Just after ... the pigeons, it was, and I thought ... oh, Tom, why didn't you tell me? Why didn't you say anything?'

'I didn't know how to.'

'You know – with your mouth! Words! Haven't you heard of them?' Her voice rose with indignation. Tom looked up at her, and smiled faintly. 'You haven't got rid of your old temper then, Mel?'

Then she felt ashamed. 'No, and I reckon I never will. Oh, you – you're so daft, Tom Farrell. Really good friends, we were, and then it all went wrong ...'

'We kept our daft brothers out of trouble, though, didn't we?' he said.

'Yes, but ...'

'I know. Look, Mel – I'm sorry I was so awful to you that day in school. I had to hit back at somebody, and you happened to be standing there. Ever since then I've wanted to say sorry, but it wouldn't come out. There wasn't the chance . . .'

'I know,' she said. 'It's OK, Tom – I knew you'd talk to me again one day.' She paused, then went on a bit sadly, 'But I didn't think it would be to tell me this. I wish you'd spoken before. There was me thinking . . . thinking . . . oh, never mind!'

'What were you thinking?'

'That you didn't *like* me anymore.'

'Talk about stupid,' he said, reaching over to take her hand, which he held very loosely between his own. 'I like you more than ever, Mel. It's just that it was very complicated, and me – I didn't want to go. At first.'

Then Tom told her the whole story, starting with meeting Lord Grafton at the prize giving, and ending with that terrible moment when he had decided – *he*, Tom – that they had to get away from Mainthorpe.

'So you wanted to go in the end?'

'Ay, I did.'

'And is it a real country cottage you'll have? Like in pictures?'

'Yeah, with roses round the door.' His voice was dry.

'Oh. Nice.'

Melanie looked down, her mouth puckering. For a while neither of them spoke. He was afraid she was going to cry and wanted her not to. There was a terrible sense of finality, which seemed slowly to be tearing the ground under him and rocking the Slab they were leaning on, in time to the pounding of his own heart.

'When are you leaving?' she asked.

'Tomorrow. Dad's hired a van. Me and him and

Jason are going to load it up later on, and we'll be off in the morning. It was cheaper that way.'

'How do you get the van back?'

'You don't have to. It's a hire firm with branches all over. Lord . . . er . . . *he* gave us the name. He's paying for it.'

'Oh.' She looked away, raising her eyebrows.

'I won't get snobby, Mel, cos I'm down there. In the south. I won't change.'

'Yes, you will,' she said. 'People always do.'

'Change?'

'Ay. We all change. Already. I mean, I'm different now, from how I was when the strike began. I didn't think much about the real world, about jobs, and strikes, and governments – but I do now. I'd rather not, but I can't help it. Sometimes it's awful. The thing is, I s'pose – we were just kids then, but we've had to grow up.'

Tom nodded, understanding completely. 'I know. I used to wish I was Linda, or a baby, you know? Not having to think. Not having to decide things. Then you could just muck about and act daft and have a good time. Funny, really. A year ago I really wanted to grow up, and now I don't.'

'Me, too. Our mum used to say "You'll be old soon enough, Melanie, don't hurry it up." But I didn't hurry it up. It hurried me up. You know, Tom, last week we went to see our Gran and she was bad, right poorly, and I thought, I don't want to get *old*. Not like that. It's *frightening*.'

He patted her hand, which had tensed as she said it. 'You'll be a grand old lady, Mel. I can see you, all in furs and diamonds and that. Oh, er . . . *if* someone'll buy them for you.'

'I'll buy them myself, thank you very much, Tom Farrell,' she retorted, with a grin.

'I bet you will too,' he said admiringly.

He looked at her. The perm had grown out now,

and he could not decide if he liked her hair better curly or straight. They chatted about the night of her perm, the night of their meeting and of the strike call – the night that had started so much.

'Doesn't it seem *ages* ago?' she sighed.

'Ay, in some ways. But I always think time goes too fast. It seems like yesterday that I asked you to go to Club with me, and I thought then . . . oh, never mind. All sorts of things. But now . . .' Tom hesitated.

'It's all over,' she finished.

'I wasn't going to say that,' he said.

'I know you weren't – but it's still true.'

They sat in silence for a while. Near them, on the ground, lay a faded bunch of chrysanthemums, a note attached to the stems. Melanie turned it over. Rain had made all the writing merge into one soft blur, but she could just make out the words, '*brave miner*'. Shrivelled petals from the bouquet blew about them.

'Oh, I nearly forgot,' said Tom, fumbling in his pocket. He pulled out a brown paper bag, folded over and over because it was too big for what it contained, and held it out to her. 'I, er . . . I bought you a present – in Doncaster Market,' he said. 'It's a sort of goodbye present.'

Surprised, and as embarrassed as he was, Melanie took it without speaking, and held it for a while in her hand. 'Open it, then,' he said.

She delved into the paper bag, and pulled out a small brown leather box, its corners battered, and the gilt trim all but worn away.

'It's only an old thing. Second-hand,' he said, 'but I really liked it. I could see you wearing it, like. But it's not much.'

Melanie could not bear the note of apology in his voice. Quickly, she opened the little box and looked. Tom's present was a little brooch. It nestled on the slightly grubby grey satin inside, and caught the light with a dull gleam. It was a flower. A small black carved flower, with leaves that stuck out each side.

'It's made of jet,' he explained eagerly.

'What's jet, Tom?' She was examining it carefully, turning it over in her hand.

'It's a sort of coal, didn't you know that? I looked it up. Rightly speaking, it's called brown coal, and yet it's black. *Jet* black, see? They used to mine it round Durham, and these parts too, I think. Used to make it into lots of jewellery in the Victorian times. Isn't that funny – to think of all these women wearing coal round their necks and on their dresses and hanging from their ears!'

'Yes, but it's not like the coal our dads mine, is it?' asked Melanie.

'I don't know. Maybe if that were cut and polished up . . .'

She held the little brooch up in front of them, twisting it again so that the jet petals shone in the rays of winter sunlight. 'Imagine,' she said softly, 'if all the coal underground looked like this, like flowers. So all they were doing was picking jet flowers out of the earth, and giving them away to everybody. It'd be right nice, wouldn't it?'

'Do you like it?' Tom asked.

Melanie looked at him, then at the piece of Victorian jewellery. It was pretty, but it was really old-fashioned – the sort of thing her Gran might have worn, before she went into hospital. Melanie thought to herself that she would probably never wear it; the girls might laugh at it . . . Yet Tom had bought it for her. Then, as she looked down at the brooch, its outline softened and broke up, and suddenly the dull sheen of the jet flower was transformed – jumping and sparkling like crystal, until she could barely see it any more. She ducked her head as if to inspect it more closely, so Tom would not see the water in her eyes.

'Ay, it's lovely. Thanks, Tom,' she murmured.

'Don't cry, Mel,' he said.

'I will if I want to!' she replied, tossing her head. And then they both laughed at that flash of the old tomboy Melanie.

Tom looked at his watch. 'I'd better go soon. They'll be bringing the van, and I haven't finished clearing my room. Our mum's so wound up she's right bad-tempered.' They both rose, packed up the rubbish, and stood on the hillside, looking down at the pithead.

'Did you ever find out, Tom – who killed your pigeons?' she asked timidly.

'No,' he said, staring back across to where the first roofs of Mainthorpe shone dully in the light. 'Dad asked around, but no one was talking. Could have been anybody down there. That's a horrible thought – or at least, it *was*. It's in the past now. It's history.'

He breathed deeply, as though relieved to be standing with the horizon all around, promising freedom. That is how it was; he knew now that for him freedom meant going away. Melanie sensed it too. And even before he had spoken she knew what he would ask her next, and what her reply would be.

'Melanie – d'you think – you'll ever move away from here? Do you think you'll ever go away to college, like we used to say?'

Melanie looked across to where the sun glinted on the stark metal structure Darren and the others had wanted to destroy – stark even against the bare and bleak fields. In her pocket, her hand curled around the little leather box that held Tom's present, the little flower made from jet-coal, which some man had once dug out of the earth. A man like her father, or her brother, or either one of her grandfathers – all slicing and digging and cutting and hauling deep down beneath the grass and trees and houses, to bring out the useful coal. Or the useless, pretty jet. Millions of them, for hundreds of years, working away and dying, sometimes – for the sake of the black stuff that the government was saying was not needed any more.

She took a deep breath too, but it expressed a different feeling to Tom's. It said that the air she was drawing in was *her* air; it was the same as her grandfather, her father and her brother were glad to breathe, when they rattled to the surface in the cage after the shift was over. It belonged to her, this air, like the landscape, and the dull little houses in Mainthorpe, and the pit itself.

'No, Tom,' she said dreamily, 'I don't think I'll ever move away. I think I'll be here for the rest of my life. And I don't mind, really.'

'Is that true, Mel? I don't believe you.'

But Tom looked at her and knew she was telling the truth. It made him sad. Yet he knew equally well that sadness was a waste of time, for both of them. Then he thought about his new school, and new friends, and the examinations he wanted to beat *everybody* in (to show that folk from the north were just as good as them) and it was like a great bursting of energy in his chest.

'Will you wear your brooch sometimes?'

'Ay, it's right nice,' she said. 'Thanks again.'

'Will you write to me sometimes?'

'I will, if you write first, Tom! I want to hear about your new school, and all that.'

'Maybe you'll come down, for a holiday.'

'Maybe I will.'

They walked down the hill, without glancing back at the gaunt memorial that meant so much to the mining community – so much that was sad and terrible, but brave, too. Just like the strike. There was no point in looking back, they both knew that instinctively.

At the bottom, by the stile, Tom paused and looked

at Melanie as if there were a million things he wanted to say, but couldn't. They both bent to pick up their bikes, and stood beside them, not wanting to move.

'Well, shall I go off first, then?' she asked, her face sad.

Tom looked up at the sky briefly, then across at her – his face suddenly bright. 'I've just thought of something, Mel.'

'What's that?'

'The strike – it's all over. It's all forgotten.'

'No. It'll never be forgotten. Never!' said Melanie stoutly.

'Oh, I know, I didn't really mean *that!* People round here will be talking about it for years yet, I know. But what I mean is, there's no sides anymore – not as far as we're concerned. You know what I mean?'

'Oh – you were thinking we couldn't be *seen* together! No – none of that matters anymore. So – right then, I'll race you.'

'No, Mel, let's *us* not race,' he said quietly, pushing himself off along the road.

And so, the two of them made the journey back together. In the sky above them a bird was hovering, hovering, searching for prey – and to it the two humans were mere specks in the landscape, disturbing its peace. Tom glanced up, and smiled to himself.

'What is it?' she asked.

'Oh, I was just thinking – I used to wander round on my own up there, and watch the birds and feel jealous of them. 'Cos they were free. But now – I dunno – I feel free, too.'

'So do I, Tom. You don't have to go away to feel free, y'know. It's your mind ... I mean, you can feel free in the same old back yard – I think.'

'Mmm.'

And after a while they stopped talking. Their silence

was companionable; there was no more need for words. Tom and Melanie just cycled along the winding road that led past the gaunt colliery, and past their school. And at last they reached the houses, not caring who might be watching. Melanie and Tom rode side by side – for the first time, and the last – right back into the centre of Mainthorpe.